Good book 12/09

PRAISE FOR THE NOVELS OF DEBORAH BEDFORD

pg 88 L.R.
Lon Ralph

WHEN YOU BELIEVE

"WHEN YOU BELIEVE gently explores the hearts of two women—one younger, one older—and the desperate secrets they keep hidden inside. . . . Deborah Bedford takes us on a journey inside those hurting hearts, plumbing their depths, seeking answers to questions we've all asked: 'Does God listen to our prayers? If He listens, does He care? If He cares, why doesn't He answer?' . . . This touching story demonstrates how carefully He listens, how much He cares, and how grace-filled are His answers."

—Liz Curtis Higgs, bestselling author of *Grace in Thine Eyes*

"Deborah Bedford spins another stirring tale, drawing the reader into the story with her trademark charm. But don't be fooled by the charm—WHEN YOU BELIEVE's innocent setting quickly becomes the cauldron for a compelling story full of pain, deceit, and ultimate redemption—a story you can't put down from start to finish. Give this one to any person who has lived in silence with secret pain."

—Patricia Hickman, author of *Painted Dresses*

"Faith and love gleam like twin jewels in WHEN YOU BELIEVE. A heartrending story of redemption and hope."

—Angela E. Hunt, author of *The Face*

more . . .

When You Believe

DEBORAH BEDFORD

New York Boston Nashville

To the ones who hide what happened even from themselves,
who don't speak of it because it just wouldn't do.
To those whose hearts have yearned to be pure before the Father.

FaithWords
Hachette Book Group
237 Park Avenue
New York, NY 10017
Visit our Web site at www.faithwords.com.

Printed in the United States of America

First edition: August 2003
Reissued: June 2009
10 9 8 7 6 5 4 3 2 1

FaithWords is a division of Hachette Book Group, Inc.
The FaithWords name and logo are trademarks of Hachette Book Group, Inc.

ISBN 978-0-446-69041-6 (pbk.)
ISBN 978-0-446-55242-4 (reissue)
LCCN: 2003104453

Cover photo of woman by Getty Images
Cover inset shot by Jupiter Images

ACKNOWLEDGMENTS

To author Sherrie Lord, who read several versions of this manuscript and made so many wise, helpful, and godly suggestions. To Natalie Stewart, whose prayers have kept me writing with joy. And to Sheila Oreskovich who, with one phone call, was always there to pray and sing Psalms over these pages. Your *thereness* means so much to me.

To Charlene Zuckerman, who made me go kayaking right when I needed it most . . . even though there *were* whitecaps on String Lake. To Maria Miller, the best neighbor anyone could wish for, who has saved me more than once during a deadline and who let me borrow the incriminating evidence found in Chapter 14.

To Pastor Mike Atkins and my family at the Jackson Hole Christian Center, because your hunger to be lovers of the Lord has taught me so much.

To Bev Elgin, counselor at Riverton High School, who

was willing to spend so many hours answering questions and giving advice.

For space, I wish to thank the staff at The Bunnery in Jackson Hole—you've kept my heart and my tea warm the entire time this piece of writing has been in the works. I also thank the staff at the Teton County Library for the comfy chair, the sunny table, and the assistance with reference books and interlibrary loans.

To my family at Hachette Book Group, each of whom works so hard to get God's message out in the right way—it is a privilege to stand beside you and to be on your team. You are each so dear to me.

To Kathryn Helmers, Agent 007, whose passion and faith and *belief* can never be replaced. May you soar with the Father, dear one. I can't wait to watch and see what the Lord will do!

To my dearest P., who read one last draft of this manuscript, and who offered so much insight. Thank you for letting me tell your story. You have awed me with your willingness to be honest before your heavenly Father and before me. I have learned so much about being *real* in front of God from you, and that, as you know, has changed my life.

The truth is incontrovertible.
Panic may resent it;
ignorance may deride it;
malice may distort it;
but there it is.

Winston Churchill

This then is how we know that we belong to the truth,
and how we set our hearts at rest in his presence
whenever our hearts condemn us.
For God is greater than our hearts, and He knows
everything.

1 John 3:18–20

CHAPTER ONE

The afternoon started like any other afternoon. The first Tuesday of October was a solid, bright school day and, outside on the school steps, the sun fell across everyone's arms like a warm shawl. The glare on Lydia's desk had veered to the left along the windowsill. She knew it was after two p.m., because the shadows of the sumac stalks outside all bent toward the east.

Lydia Porter had been in her cubicle at Shadrach High School ever since the second lunch bell. She still had three months to work on this Missouri standards-test schedule, and it would take her that long to figure it out. If the juniors and seniors tested upstairs, she'd been thinking, the sophomores could take over B-hall downstairs. But that would leave a quarter of this year's freshmen wandering around A-hall after third period with nothing to do.

Her biggest challenge every year, this test schedule. She

propped her chin in her palm and stared at her notes. That's when the timid *tap-tap-tapping* began at the counseling office door.

"Come in."

The door opened five inches and a teenager's head appeared in the crack. Amazing how the young ladies always acted so hesitant, when the boys just burst in.

A little wave, an uncertain smile. "Miss P?"

"Hey, Shelby. How are you?"

For the moment, the teenager left the door open behind her. Halls that in nine minutes would be coursing with students—friends shouting, conversation rising—stood empty. Rows of beige metal lockers waited, closed. Except for the hum of incandescent lights in the ceiling and the far, muted voice of someone's emphatic lecture in a classroom, the building was quiet.

"I'm . . . I'm okay. Well, I guess."

Lydia's chair rolled over the plastic floor mat with a welcoming clatter. "So, how's that leg?"

Shelby had gotten hurt tripping up the goalie from Osceola in the third game of the season. Since then, everybody had teased her about how, for a gentle and sweet girl, she'd been getting downright mean on the soccer field.

"It's getting better."

"That's good."

"Yeah." A pause, while they studied each other. "Miss P? You got a minute?"

"Sure I do. Come on in. What's up?"

"I was hoping . . . maybe . . . we could talk."

"I'd love to."

In Shelby came, her messy bun sprouting from her crown like a rhododendron and her sunglasses perched high atop her head. She pulled up a chair, adjusted her tiny skirt, and sat. She stayed a good minute with her knees together and her feet splayed apart, her clog-toes tapping the ground.

She fiddled with the engraved nameplate on Lydia's desk that read, "Miss Porter. School-to-Careers Counselor."

"So," Lydia asked in a light voice, slapping her legs with her hands, settling in. "You been thinking about colleges lately?"

"No, not really."

Shelby Tatum was one of Lydia's favorites. She was one of those lucky kids whose mother showed up at every parent/teacher conference, giving proof to their favorite dictum in this office: the parents who showed up at teacher's conferences were seldom the parents who needed to. Recently, Shelby's grandfather had sold an old house down in Barry County and her parents had let him build a guesthouse on their property. Such a blessing; most kids never even got to know their grandfathers. And Shelby's stepdad parked himself on the sidelines of every soccer game, roaring his approval of her team. Every week he'd be there with his golf umbrella, a folding chair, and a dilapidated briefcase as wide as a corn-fed piglet, filled with documents from Place-Perfect Missouri Real Estate, where he worked.

So college wasn't the right button to push. Well, she

was only a sophomore. Lydia probed a little further. "Your classes coming along okay?"

"Yeah," the girl said. "Okay."

Over the past year Shelby had sealed Lydia's admiration by launching into those loose, comfortable conversations in the hall. Not the way adults launched into them, mind you, but the way only a sixteen-year-old would do it: stony silent if you dared ask questions, burbling torrents of information when you least expected it.

That's why it seemed odd today, after the door shut quietly behind them, that Shelby didn't have anything to say.

Lydia's pointed questions, Shelby's short, vague answers, fizzled into silence.

A heavy breath lifted Shelby's breastbone and set it down again. Her eyes had taken on an unfathomable hue, a darkness that made Lydia lean forward.

No, I can see. It's more troubling than school stuff.

She waited for Shelby to volunteer something. She knew she had to be willing to wait. This girl who normally gestured largely to her friends in the hallway, who slumped against her locker chattering on her cell phone, now sat with her chin against her collarbone, a twist of hair fallen from her bun, hiding her face. As she studied her, Lydia noticed the swollen eyes, the smudges beneath them as dark as slashes of purple lipstick. She had never seen Shelby this distressed.

Oh my.

Lydia felt a draw toward the girl so strong and natural

that it might have been a tide in the ocean or the pull of the moon. She cared so much about all of them, especially the discomfited ones—the ones who had pushed boundaries a little too hard, the ones broken and flailing out against people, who didn't understand how worthy they were.

A sense of warm purpose welled in her bosom.

How she longed to touch these kids with her heart, to share with them real tools for living instead of the slick pages of college catalogs.

It's the future you see in this place, never the present, Lydia thought. Never the present, until a worried student comes walking in the door.

Now that Lydia thought about it, she remembered Amy Mera mentioning that Shelby, usually a stellar student, had missed homework in history. She hadn't finished a French II assignment, either.

So she asked, "You've been having trouble keeping up in class?"

Besides soccer, Shelby sang in honor choir, had been picked to be on the mock trial team, and came early for meetings of the student council. And, as everyone knew, the good kids could get way too busy.

Shelby had kept her backpack slung by one strap over her shoulder. Now, she let it slip to the floor between her legs. "If I had problems in one of my classes," she asked as she replaced Lydia's nameplate on the desk and reached for a paperclip instead, "could you help me?"

"Of course I could. We could get you into a study hall

fifth period. We could find you a tutor for French II if you needed it."

"That's all it would take to get you to help me with something, Miss P? To tell you about it?"

"Yes."

"I want to tell you about it," Shelby said, "because you're the only one I can talk to."

Lydia nodded, waited.

"You're the only one who's really listened to me for a long time."

Lydia waited some more.

"Well." Shelby's fingernails, painted a *Glamour*-magazine buff, had been chewed on. With them, she bent the paper-clip into the shape of an elongated S and dropped it on the desktop. "Really, it's nothing."

"It is that, then? Do you need a tutor?"

They listened to each other breathing for a while.

"No, it isn't that, either."

Another dead end. Well, Lydia knew how to find her way around dead ends. She began to try a little harder. "Things okay with your peers? Everything okay between you and your friends?"

"Yeah." The girl cocked her head. "Everything's fine."

"So, everything okay at home?"

At that moment the door burst open and in barreled three uninvited boys. "Hey, Miss P," Tommy Ballard announced as the door hit the wall. "My mom said I was supposed to stop by here and pick up something."

"Tommy—"

"Don't remember what it was, though."

Lydia resented the interruption, but tried to sound reasonable. "Are you going to be out? Homework, maybe?"

"No. Something else."

"You know the rules around here, don't you? When you come into this office, you're supposed to knock. We were talking."

"Oh." Lydia saw Tommy glance with interest at Shelby. "Sorry."

Shelby surveyed the weave of the industrial carpet beside her left clog as if it were the most intriguing pattern she'd ever laid eyes on. She looked like she wanted to disappear into thin air.

"What are you doing in here, Shelb?"

"None of your business, Ballard."

"Tommy—"

"Oh." He snapped his fingers. "I know what I needed. Is this where we get those SAT sign-up things?"

"Over there."

"Thanks."

In the same way they'd burst in with no regard, the boys overzealously helped themselves to what they needed. They started out before Lydia finished. "And this is the book of sample questions on the test," she called as she held out another pamphlet. "You boys knock next time."

Tommy seized the booklet from her hand, rolled it inside

his palm, and smacked the doorjamb with it. "See you, Shelb." He led his tribe of friends out the door.

Wordlessly, they watched Tommy Ballard go. Lydia readjusted herself, settled in the chair. Shelby played with a buckle on her backpack.

Lydia tried again after the silence seemed like it had gone on forever. "You didn't answer my question, Shelby. Is everything okay at home?"

Shelby tossed her head so one strand of unrestrained hair flew back against her shoulder and then fell forward again. Her shoulders slumped against the back of the chair. Lydia saw her slight hesitation. The girl's lips parted as if she wanted to say something. Then they shut again.

Shelby grappled on the floor for her backpack. "I've got to go."

Lydia couldn't lose her now. If she did, Shelby might be gone completely. She might disappear into the river of students that coursed toward their next classes when the bell rang.

With a sinking heart, she tacked a different direction, broaching the subject the way someone would check a tender bruise. "You're frightened. I can tell that much."

"Why do you say that?"

"Because you want to run away."

"I—I can't do this."

"But you're here. You came because you wanted to talk."

The girl rose, upsetting the nameplate on the desk. "I said I've got to go."

"Shelby." Lydia reached for her arm and grabbed her, but didn't rise. To rise would have meant concession, and she wouldn't do that.

"It doesn't matter."

"It does."

Silence.

"Sit down."

"I can't do it."

Lydia searched her mind for something, anything, that might change the girl's decision to leave. "Don't let Tommy Ballard mess this up."

They stared each other down. At last, Shelby plopped back into the chair and dropped her backpack again.

"Okay," Lydia said. "Let's start over."

Outside the counseling-office window, a sprinkler kicked out its traveling arc of water over grass that looked as shorn and sun cured as a drill sergeant's haircut. The letter board proclaimed in four-inch red-and-blue capitals GO FIRE-RATTLERS! 1999 MISSOURI STATE CLASS 2A CHAMPS.

Underneath, smaller type declared *Homecoming Dance, Oct. 10, A Night To Remember.*

"It's hard, you know."

"Whatever it is that's happened, Shelby, there's probably a way to make it right."

"Not this."

"Try me."

9

"Sometimes there's things that are just . . . impossible to tell."

Folks in St. Clair County, Missouri, liked to say that Lydia Porter had once had a gift. When she'd been a little girl, she'd been able to take her father's hand, lead him into the hill country, and find deer hunters who had lost their way. They'd written up a story about her in the weekly *Shadrach Democrat Reflex* when she'd been ten and her father had brought her here to visit her Uncle Cy—the year Eddy Sandlin had turned up missing during Cub Scout Troup 517's day hike.

She'd helped find him sitting on a beaver dam in Yesterday Creek, snagging driftwood with his feet.

They said she did it by listening to the trees. They said she walked along through the forest at the edge of town, guiding her way through the dusk, touching the heels of her palms against the shaggy, rough bark of the hickory and the smooth, overlapping blue-gray mottles of the sycamore, listening. Letting something bigger than herself guide her, thinking maybe it could be the Lord who whispered to her. For a long time, she'd been willing to hear Him with an innocent child's ears.

They said she heard things that grownups wouldn't let themselves hear anymore.

But that sort of thing hadn't happened to Lydia Porter in a very long time. Except for the yellowed newspaper clipping her mother kept pressed in the family scrapbook between faded Polaroids of Border collie pups and her first communion, Lydia could hardly even remember.

Lydia had learned to rely on other things now. She relied on asking the right questions.

And so she kept asking questions now. "If there isn't something wrong at home, is it anything to do with the boys?"

A bloom of color burned Shelby's cheeks. Lydia knew she was on to something. She tried to see into the girl's downcast eyes. "Is that it? Boys?"

The girl clenched her fist in her lap. "No." Then she unclenched it again. "Maybe." Tears glossed her waxy lashes. One escaped and ran down, leaving behind a track of eyeliner. "I keep thinking maybe it's something I've done. Maybe it's something I've said to him to make him think—"

Lydia watched Shelby try to focus her attention anywhere but on a counselor's face. She watched her stare at the square letters on the sign beside the desk that read LACK OF PLANNING ON YOUR PART DOES NOT CONSTITUTE AN EMERGENCY ON MY PART. She watched her play with the tiny gold promise ring on her left hand, with its almost-invisible diamond chip. She watched her snuffle and wipe her nose on the back of her wrist.

"Well," Shelby said at last, "you know there's Sam Leavitt." In distress, she stopped and began to wiggle the ring back and forth until the tiny stone captured a prism of sunlight from the window. The reflection moved like a flitting bug against the wall.

"You want to finish that sentence?"

"I'm in family science this semester, you know."

"I know."

"W-we talked about abstinence, how it was the best thing to do to keep your body healthy, to be pure. We talked about signing a *contract*."

A tear fell onto Shelby's hands. Another onto her jeans. Then another, leaving wet splotches on her denim the size of nickels.

"See, I told you there wasn't anything anybody could do."

"That contract makes you uncomfortable?"

"I c-can't sign something like that. Not after what's—" The girl tucked her elbows hard against her ribcage and moaned. "Sam wouldn't ever want somebody like m-me."

Instinctively, Lydia moved toward her. She was caught off guard by the flare of terror in Shelby's eyes. Shelby tucked up her body to protect herself, warding Lydia off with her hands. Lydia was stunned. Hastily, she withdrew to the other side of the desk. "You can't think that about yourself. Why would you?"

Their eyes met.

"Have you been"—how to pursue this, to be respectful and gentle with a child who had, perhaps, lost her innocence?—"*active* with someone? With this boy you like? Or with someone else?"

"No." The girl's answer came quick and sharp. "No, of course not." Then, "Not exactly."

"Well, what do you mean by that? Have you and this boy done some things?"

Even as she asked the question, Lydia was afraid. *Say yes, Shelby. Yes. Because anything else means something unthinkable is going on.*

"Oh no." The tears came fresh and Shelby's voice broke with regret. "No . . . no . . . no . . . no, no."

Lydia leaned to the edge of her chair, her mouth gone dry with dread. Suddenly she began to understand. "Is it someone else, then? Someone else being inappropriate with you? An adult?"

No nod. No answer. Just a bitten lower lip, eyes that seemed to stare through the floor, tears streaming down the face of a girl who had always seemed so happy. Just the desperate, broken expression of a young lady with her shoulders shaking, who twenty minutes ago had seemed to have everything in the world on her side.

Shelby found a gash in her fingernail and bit a sliver of it away, leaving raw, pink skin at the quick.

"Shelby?"

The girl covered her mouth and gasped like she was going to be sick. That one helpless gurgle told Lydia everything she needed to know.

Lydia went numb, the silent air pounding heavy against her ears.

Everybody in Shadrach knew everybody else. Surely no

one in this little town would be capable of something like that.

"You want to give a name, honey? You've got to tell me who's doing this and"—she followed her professional training now, no leading with her words, no power of suggestion—"bothering you."

"I c-can't."

"You can." Lydia struggled against her own frantic need to press. *Keep this girl safe. Keep this girl at ease, and talking.* "I need you to tell me."

Shelby was an achiever, a girl they'd all known since she'd first learned to write in cursive and do long division and run the right direction on a soccer field. If there was someone capable of touching a teenager inappropriately in this town, the folks of Shadrach would find him out, punish him, put him away.

"Then everybody will know, and he said . . . he said . . ."

"It's hard, Shelby. But it's important. It's appropriate that you would tell someone."

". . . he said if they found out, nobody would believe me anyway. That they'd blame *me* for what happened."

From the hall came the wakening sounds of Shadrach High School as the minutes moved toward the bell—the hoots of girls in the corridor; a reprimand from a voice she recognized as Maureen Eden's; the stale, wet-bread smell from the cafeteria creeping under the door. A door opened and, through the window to the hallway, Lydia could see the blue plastic easel with brochures that read JOIN THE AIR FORCE. AIM HIGH.

"He said if I told, he would say I was lying. He said something horrible would happen to me."

"We can only keep you safe if you'll let us help you."

"I just want . . . I w-want it to stop."

"If you want it to stop, Shelby, you have to give a name. You can't protect him."

The girl sounded as if she were trying to speak through a gag. But she repeated herself, and the meaning sank in. "I-I'm scared."

"We're not going to let him hurt you. Do you understand that?"

Shelby shook her head again. No.

Who? Who would want to do this? Who would do this to some young girl who just wanted to stay pure?

"If you'll just tell me—"

A meeting of eyes.

"—who did it."

Silence. Shelby leaned all her weight onto her hands. "He's going to say it was me. He's going to say he didn't do it. That everybody ought not to believe me."

"If you'll just tell me what went on, we can keep this man from . . . from *hassling* you again."

"He . . . he touches me when I don't want him to. And he makes me touch him back."

"You have to tell me who this is." Lydia knew she was pushing, but she couldn't hold herself back any longer.

15

Hearing these things, she couldn't keep herself from pressing on.

Shelby stared out the window as if she was uncertain what to do next. Out of the corner of her eye, Lydia noticed a shadow, probably one of the teachers walking by outside. Shelby studied the person walking by outside. She studied her thumbnail, first one angle, then another. Finally, after all that waiting, she said it so quickly that Lydia almost didn't realize what was happening. She spoke in a child's voice, telling secrets.

"M-Mr. Stains. It was him."

Lydia took a full five seconds to realize what she'd heard.

The first blow, when she understood Shelby wasn't accusing someone in the community. She was accusing someone in the *school.*

The second blow, when her brain registered his name.

For one of the few times in her life, Lydia experienced a physical reaction to words. Adrenaline jolted through her, deserted her, leaving her faint. The silence roared. She couldn't think past the ringing in her ears.

"Who?" she asked, her voice gone weak. "Who did you say?"

But she had heard. At his name, something war-torn and leaden had taken hold in her chest.

"You heard me, didn't you?" Shelby said, holding up the second thumbnail to compare it with the first. "You know who he is?"

In the silence, Lydia made a choking noise. Step by step into the dark journey she went, the weight of horror pitching forward and slamming her. Not Charles Stains.

Lydia stared hopelessly at the empty ring finger on her left hand. "Yes. Yes, of course I do know him."

"The woodshop teacher."

"I know who you're talking about."

"The one everybody calls 'Mr. S.'"

"I know who he is, Shelby."

On the outside, her words sounded as calm as a lapping lakeshore evening, the precise moment of stillness as the stars set in and the breeze dies away.

On the inside, Lydia felt as roiled up and out-of-control as the water that churned between the bluffs of Viney Creek.

No. Oh, please, God. No.

Oh, no no no.

Let it be anybody but Charlie.

CHAPTER TWO

—— ✑ ——

*F*olks in Shadrach, Missouri, liked to say their town had high ground and low ground, with nothing much in between.

Along the northeast edge of town, where fingers of Brownbranch Lake poked between high hills, bald eagles chose the heights to build their nests. In the lowlands that fell off to the south, the mist sank and skirted each swell of land, dropping heavy as maple syrup into each draw.

From the high places to the low places, from the crests of the sycamore trees to the tangled brambles of hawthorn and Sweet William in the bottomlands, the sun never really got the chance to sift through.

"This Shadrach land," a travel journalist from the *Kansas City Star* had written once, "is nothing more than a mess of hollers and knobs."

Yes, Lydia thought. A person was either always standing

at the top looking down or standing at the bottom looking up. There was no such thing as level ground in St. Clair County.

When Lydia had visited as a girl, it was her Uncle Cy who had always brought her here to this place, from his old clapboard house on the hill to the gloss-smooth lake that lay below it. On the water, Cy had taught her how to coax the decrepit Evinrude motors to life on the rental boats. She had yanked the cord until her small arm throbbed, then twisted open the throttle so the ancient outboard could sputter to life. When the engine caught, the air billowed with acrid, blue smoke. Then the water slid away beneath the hull like murky, satin skin, alive above the propeller.

Lydia had learned long, long ago to take her problems to the Brownbranch.

A fifteen-minute drive carried her east from the high school to the marina. Her decade-old LeSabre crunched on the gravel and, when she turned the engine off, above its hot ticking she heard only the chortling of scaups and mallards, the lapping of wavelets against the shore.

She climbed out and looked around for somebody. "Uncle Cy? Jane?"

Cy hadn't paid much attention to women after Lydia's Aunt Donna had died. Until Jane Cabbot stumbled up onto Cy Porter's doorstep one rainy afternoon seven years ago, looking to rent a boat, and never left. Soon they had become a couple and later they'd married. Lydia thought it mildly romantic when she watched them gassing up and hiring out motorboats together, coaxing the outboards with language she hadn't known people like Cy and Jane understood. Together they sifted through damp dirt in search of the most luscious night crawlers. They sold wooden plaques carved with jokes and mottos, fishing licenses and Spin-a-Lures and stink bait. They pointed out the Polaroid photos on the wall labeled with the length and weight of bass that had come out of the lake, pictures of fish carcasses and bodies—all remembrances of that one summer in 1979 when someone had a camera.

Of course those people in the photos were long gone. But, no matter. It was the fish everybody wanted to talk about anyway.

Lydia watched the couple with yearning every time Jane skirted the display of Rapala reels and gave her uncle a fond pop on the rump with her chamois. And every time Lydia saw the tender expression in Jane's eyes when she sidled up next to her husband behind the cash register, laid a possessive hand on his shoulder and announced, "There's not anybody I know who can sink a bait hook better than Cy Porter." Each time Lydia thought, *Surely God intended for someone to love me that way. Surely there's somebody in the world God wanted me to have, too.*

Lydia was proud of being a Porter. "Like a porter on a train," she'd heard her father introduce himself dozens of times. And nothing had seemed more exotic and exciting when she had been a little girl than that—being named after a porter who worked on an eastbound train all the way to Providence, on the westbound train clear through Missouri into Kansas, a man whose face shone like rock polished in a tumbler, deft gloved fingers barely touching the tickets while he nicked their corners with a punch.

Nothing had seemed that exotic or exciting, that is, until Maureen Eden, the school nurse, began gossiping about Charlie Stains in the teacher's lounge last year.

"When he was a kid, all he wanted to do was get out of this place." Maureen had stood in the doorway with a CPR mannequin draped like a carcass over her arms. "Now, why on earth would an English Lit professor come back to teach woodshop in Shadrach?"

"How are you doing, Mo?" the art teacher asked. "You're supposed to talk about yourself before you walk in and start talking about somebody else."

"I'm losing my mind is how I'm doing. I was on my way for something and I don't remember what." With the entire length of rubber body, Maureen gestured her loss.

"Anything to do with"—Lydia nodded toward the mannequin—"that?"

Maureen had stared down at it as if she'd never seen it before. "Oh, yeah. Wiley wanted this. I was taking it down to vocational. Health occupations." She sighed and turned to leave. "What can I say? I'm going through menopause. I live in the present because I can't remember what happened five minutes in the past."

"Everybody around here has known Charlie forever."

"It's good he's coming home."

21

"Charlie Stains was a professor? At a college?"

Everyone nodded. "University of Missouri. In St. Louis."

"Left here the year he graduated from Shadrach and said he never intended to be back."

"Hm-mmm. Well, you know the only thing that's ever constant is change. Maybe Charlie needed a change of life, too."

"That's what he thought he was getting when he left here."

"Anybody see him downtown? He doesn't *look* like a college professor."

"Well, he doesn't look like a woodshop teacher, either."

Lydia had opened the refrigerator door and searched the aluminum shelves for the raspberry yogurt she'd brought in yesterday.

Mo said, "My dad has known the family forever. Good people. Such a nice young man, he says. You can't have too many people like Charlie around."

"Still, it's interesting." Brad Gritton, the journalism teacher, also worked as a freelance reporter for the *Shadrach Democrat Reflex*. They teased him at the school all the time about being a fact worshiper. "When you don't know what somebody's been doing all these years . . ."

Lydia's yogurt had vanished. Somebody had eaten it. She shut the refrigerator with a little snap. "So, you tell us, Mo. What's a woodshop teacher supposed to look like?"

Maureen rose to the challenge. "He's supposed to look

22

like Dave Whitsitt when he was framing in the snack bar at Fire-Rattler Stadium. You know, with his knuckles bunged up, scabs on his arms, and his hair all full of sawdust. You've seen woodworkers' hands before. Rough as Taum Sauk Mountain."

"Hands. Now that's what I notice about a man first. Big, wide, working hands." Patrice Saunders warmed her fingers around her favorite coffee mug, with TEACHERS DO IT WITH CLASS emblazoned all the way around. "You just get to see those other things, Mo, because you're the school nurse."

That's when they turned to Lydia with a conspiratorial expression in their eyes, as if they'd just realized the possibility; all of them except Brad Gritton.

"What about you?" Mo asked. Smiles passed around. No matter what Charlie Stains had come back for or what he'd been doing, they each knew that a new man in town might mean a new chance for Lydia. "What do you notice first in a man, Lydia?"

Five pairs of eyes had locked onto her.

"I don't know," she said, staring them down.

Jean Lowder aligned her latest pop quiz in the copier. The machine began to click and whirr, and pages began to feed out of the other side like a pile of drifting feathers. "First thing I noticed about my husband was his Adam's apple," she said. "Darney was out on the basketball court in Springfield and I thought, 'That boy's got the biggest

Adam's apple I've ever seen.' It was even knobbier than his knees."

∽

THE SIGHT OF her uncle's AM radio on the steps brought Lydia back that Tuesday evening. Such a simple thing, with its bent antenna and its Panasonic speaker that looked like the underside of a George Lucas star-cruiser.

Every day at Viney Creek Marina, Lydia's uncle held court surrounded by friends, in a row of musty aluminum chairs, the plastic webbing sagging in the middle from years of use. Now the chairs were empty. She peered into the darkness of the weatherworn boathouse and squinted, willing her eyes to adjust.

"Uncle Cy? You around?"

Skeletal remains of a gear case lay in disarray on the floor. A dented propeller listed beside a handful of tools. Behind her, three aluminum fishing boats rocked on their moorings beside a wharf new enough to still reek of cedar.

The sun already cast long shadows. Lydia knew she didn't have much time. She thumped a battered gas tank to see if it was full.

It wasn't.

Slowly, she fed in the premix, listening to the *glub glubbing,* hearing the pitch rise as liquid closed in toward the top.

Charlie is my life now, Lord. I thought that's why You made this happen between us. I don't understand. I can't turn any other way.

24

Then she thought, *If he's done something, if he's touched Shelby, it will ruin him.* She did not dare think, *If I tell.*

Just as she lugged the tank to the waterfront and climbed in over the algae-covered fenders, Uncle Cy came around the ancient Coca-Cola chest on the sunset side of the marina. He hollered at her across the collar of rocks and sand.

"Lyddie?"

From the rocking, moored boat, she cupped her hands around her mouth to answer. "Hey."

"Where you going?"

"Oh—" She shrugged, standing straddle legged. "Humbert's Finger, I guess."

"It's late to be going out that far."

"I'll be okay." She attached her tank to the fuel line of the Evinrude, squeezed the primer bulb once, twice, and pulled out the choke. "You mind?"

"Course I don't."

"Charlie called out here a while ago. Wanted to know where you were."

"Oh." *Oh.*

Three pulls on the starter and the engine coughed, caught, rattled to life. She reversed, banked the metal skiff into a sharp one-eighty as the low sun illuminated rocks beneath water the same russet-red as a robin's breast. She waved to her uncle and headed away.

Usually Lydia hugged the shore until she passed Viney Creek Point. This afternoon she steered into open water, running the throttle wide open, the motor churning a fine spray behind her. For the first time since Shelby had mentioned Mr. Stains's name in her office three hours ago, Lydia felt as if she could breathe.

She rode the bucking waves the way she rode her bucking emotions. To keep herself steady, she locked her eyes on the opposite bank, where the high-water mark descended into the lake like broad, shadowed steps.

We can only keep you safe, she'd said to Shelby, *if you'll let us help you.*

Charles Stains had sauntered into the first teacher's meeting of the year with hands as smooth and big around as rutabagas, a clipped, careful accent from the opposite side of the state, and rich twill trousers—all of this rare and unfamiliar and somewhat questionable in Shadrach. During the full first six months of class, in which his students turned black-oak limbs into candlesticks on the school-district lathe, learned the intricate art of handrubbed finishes on wobbly napkin holders, and built unsteady spice cabinets from planks of hickory, he had remained half welcomed and half suspected by them all.

One Tuesday afternoon late in the spring, he had turned up at Cy Porter's.

He'd waited in line for his turn at the marina cash register. As he scribbled down his phone number, Lydia noticed his fingers were torn by splinters and his cuticles dyed brown with mahogany stain.

"How would you feel about my carpentry students rebuilding your dock, Mr. Porter?"

"Don't know about that," Lydia overheard while she helped Jane unload a cardboard box of trolling spoons. "One I've got out there seems fine."

"I didn't say it wasn't." The mysterious professor picked up a Snickers bar from the counter and laid down three quarters. "But it seemed like an idea. I've got a lot of faith in these kids. They could do a good job."

"Well, you just take another look out there. Tell me why you think I need something better than what I've already got."

"Folks everywhere are putting in those galvanized metal docks that move with the waves. I'd hate to see you do that. My kids would learn a lot, updating what you've got now." Stains tore open one end of the Snickers and bit into it. "There's just something about a wooden dock," he said around the glob of chocolate and peanuts in his mouth. "It adds to the atmosphere of a place."

Cy pushed the cash drawer shut.

"You build it, son, you got to guarantee it. I'm not paying one red cent to fix something if you go crazy and mess things up."

It had been a big project from the very beginning, the seniors hauling in treated redwood and cedar in the bed of Johnny Nagle's rusty Dodge Power Wagon, the juniors saying that *they* ought to be the ones who got to go waist deep in water to extract rotted pilings from the mud.

"Why are you doing this?" Lydia had asked him one evening when she'd gone to deliver groceries to Jane. She'd found Charlie wearing an unlikely ragged T-shirt with the sleeves cut off, tightening huge bolts that must have still been hot from the sun.

She stood on shore as if she was afraid to set foot on the planks he'd laid. He torqued down with his pliers, the muscles in his shoulders twisting like cables of wet hemp rope.

"I've been studying this, Mr. Stains," she announced to his sunburned shoulders, "and I think you're out to prove something to somebody. Only I can't figure out what, or who."

He torqued down harder.

"Pardon me for saying it, but it seems like you're trying to rebuild something that you don't need to rebuild."

"Why does everybody think I've got to have some reason?"

"We're just trying to figure out who you are."

"Well, I'm Charlie. That's who I am and I wish you'd call me that." He laid down the pliers. "Who you see is who you get."

"I guess I was one of the only people in town who didn't live here when you did. I just made it out for summers as a kid."

His blistered shoulders rose and fell. "You know he would have put in a metal pier eventually." Finally, he turned halfway toward her. "And metal docks spook the fish. Minnows don't like them as well, either. The pylons need to be low in the water. Moss needs to grow."

"Uncle Cy's always liked wooden docks."

"You ever do any night fishing? You ever come out here at midnight and see what the crappie will do when they see the light?"

"Used to," she told him. "My uncle and I used to come out here all the time. No more, though. Don't have time for late nights anymore, now that I'm at the school."

Without meeting her eyes, he hefted himself over the side and splashed thigh-deep in water. He retrieved his tools, waded out, and worked his way under the hewn lumber. He went at the nuts and bolts from beneath.

"You ever think I might be rebuilding this dock so I'd get an honest chance to talk to you?"

His words surprised and flattered her. In one quick moment, she couldn't help comparing him to Brad Gritton, the other single teacher at the school, who had been trying to date her ever since she'd been hired on at Shadrach. Brad had even asked her to the *Shadrach Democrat Reflex* Christmas party last December. She'd turned him down, wanting to be fair. Brad, who had always seemed like more of a buddy than someone she could be passionate about, with his self-conscious habit of retucking his shirt every few minutes and his affinity for verifiable and undistorted fact.

Charlie said, "There's nobody out here but you and me. We aren't at Shadrach High School today."

"No, we aren't."

She wondered what he meant to do about that. For a

long time, they stood silent. Then, "Can you hand me that extra pair of pliers? I forgot and left them up there."

"Sure. Here you are."

Finally she set foot on the dock. When she poked the tool between the planks of cedar, their hands touched.

Hands, someone had said in the teacher's lounge. *I always notice a man by his hands.*

The rubber handle grips wouldn't fit between the boards. She pulled them back out again. Deep inside, Lydia, a woman who longed to be cherished and needed by someone, to be found beautiful by someone, felt her heart begin to unclench. She climbed over the side with the pliers, into the water. Dozens of minnows darted away from her in an odd, ordered formation.

The cold water bit into her skin, gave her gooseflesh, exhilarated her. It smelled of duckweed and fish and diesel. For a moment, she braided her arms across her midriff, as if to protect herself from him and the cold water both.

Such a crazy thing, being this pleased and spontaneous. She would never have done anything so impulsive with anyone else. Certainly not with Brad, who asked too many questions and was interested only in precise details and data.

"Here." She unfolded her arms and waggled the pliers over her head at him, her heart pounding. "You want these?"

"That depends."

"On what?"

He came around the corner of the dock and sloshed to-ward her. "On whether you're willing to give them to me or not."

Lydia stood still holding the pliers overhead, waiting for him as he moved between the moored boats. Brownbranch water rushed against her when he came close and brushed against her, the hem of his shirt scalloping like the edge of a jelly fish. And there, in the waning sunset, waist-deep in water with their wet clothes clinging, the much-talked-about Professor Charlie Stains took the liberty of kissing her.

He felt his way at first, questioning her with his mouth but not his arms, his hands poised skyward as if somebody in a Western had said "Stick 'em up." He kissed her with-out committing anything, as if wanting to give her an easy chance to step away.

She didn't.

And so, he kissed her again.

His lips . . . yes, she'd thought about them and wondered how they would feel on hers. Sometimes when she'd seen him at Shadrach High, his mouth had been so cracked and chapped that she'd wanted to offer him her Blistex. But for now his lips were as wet as the rest of him, a surprise, soft and cool where she'd thought they'd be rough and dry, and pink-red in a way she'd never seen them before.

She didn't feel self-conscious as he gripped her shoulders. Charlie seemed so sure of what he was doing. His belt had turned dark in the water. She loved the way she felt small as he drew her against him. Maybe, she realized, she was more than pleased and flattered. Maybe this could be what she had been praying for. And here she stood against Charlie's sodden belt buckle in her red-print dress with spaghetti straps—the one that made her feel less like an aging teacher and more like a girl in springtime.

Oh Lord Oh Lord Oh Lord.

There had been a hole in her heart for so long. Since she'd been in high school, she had never thought that she deserved to be loved this way.

"I could do this," she'd said to him very quietly that day. "I could."

Tuesday evening, only thirty minutes since Shelby had left her office and, already, all that had changed. She held her course in the lake, not hurrying to Humbert's Finger. The moment she took herself to the protection of a cove, the moving water wouldn't carry her anymore. For the next few hours at least, she would bear Shelby's disclosure alone.

She waited until breakers began to slop up over the ribs of the boat. She waited until her feet got wet before she throttled up the Evinrude and headed into the narrow, protected inlet. The boat stilled as she passed between two ridges. It glided on a mirror. Farther ahead, at the edge of the bay, an old, abandoned house, its porch overgrown with hawthorn, sat on cleared ground in the shape of a warbler's wing. No road could be seen in or out, only a faint track choked with brambles and milkweed.

She'd walked these paths often during the months she and Charlie had quietly fallen in love. *Thank you thank you thank you God,* she'd whispered over and over again as she searched the sky, the reflections in the water, for Him. *You heard me, didn't you? You knew what I'd wanted above all things.*

Because, at the bottom of everything else, she stood on her faith. The Lord was somebody she talked to and sought and asked questions of. She looked for answers in His Word. She knew He had created her to need someone loving her and standing beside her. She had always told others how she could trust Him.

Evening was coming on, heralded by the ringing throb of crickets and cicadas that had survived the early October frosts. On the sand at the far edge of the inlet, she made out the hump of an enormous lake turtle lying almost invisible against the rocks.

Motionless, finally, away from the discord of voices. Away from lockers slamming like cymbals in the hallway. Away from Shelby Tatum's horrid story and her eyes, as desperate and as sad as death.

One evening. One sunset alone on the Brownbranch to deliberate and, she knew, a state court could already charge her with negligence.

One still hour while she weighed the misery in her heart with the fresh gift of what had been given her with the graveness of a girl's claim.

Shelby Tatum could have gone to anyone. But she knew she was safe, coming to me.

Along the shore of Humbert's Finger the water had turned from blue to penny-gilded copper. If Lydia didn't head toward the point now, she wouldn't make the marina before dark. She saw the silhouette of someone kneel down and then get up again, holding the enormous lake turtle aloft by the shell.

Behind the figure holding the turtle, another person wadded newspapers and pumped a metal lighter-fluid can over a stack of driftwood. The flicker of a match, and a bonfire erupted. People always did this in Shadrach. Probably high school kids partying on the shore.

From far away the fire looked beautiful. Driftwood burned in its own elegant shapes, the flames as graceful as a dancer's arms. She imagined Charlie's face in the dancing shadows. Remembered his expression when he'd lifted the box from Hocklander's Jewelry and handed it to her like it had been a nagging child tugging at his pocket.

I can't stand it any longer.

Can't stand what, Charlie?

Wondering what you're going to say.

About what?

About this.

This what?

I'd planned to buy you a sundae after the game and put this inside the whipped cream. But I was afraid you would eat the ring.

What ring? What are you talking about?

There had been no need to whisper, even though they were. Above them the Friday-night game had packed the football stadium. From where they stood in the dark beneath the bleachers, everything around them seemed to roar.

What are you doing?

Lydia Louise Porter, what do you think I'm doing? I'm asking you to marry me.

Right now?

Yes. Right now. And if you don't watch out, some of our own students are going to sneak under here to neck and they're going to find us instead.

They don't call it necking anymore, do they? Is it all over town that my middle name is Louise?

If you don't like this ring, we can take it back, but it looked like you, and I wanted to pick it out and I thought it might be better to do it here so everybody in Shadrach won't know by tomorrow morning and . . . and . . . we've waited too long, both of us. Lyddie, would you just open it up?

Her answer had been *yes yes yes*, and the ring, given so quickly, had been tucked away in its velvet Hocklander's box for the past four long, careful days. They'd decided to live with their gentle secret awhile because it would be such a huge point of discussion once the teenagers found out. It would be amazing for the kids, they'd decided. They'd have to learn to call her Mrs. S instead of Miss P.

Not even Maureen Eden knew yet—not Mo, who prized

herself on knowing everything and sharing it with glee in the nurses' office and the teacher's lounge.

Nor did her parents, who resided in their comfortable colonial home in Lichen Bridge, Connecticut. Just last week Lydia had been an hour on the phone with American Airlines, juggling her schedule so she and Charlie could get tickets together into Hartford over Christmas break. How joyful her parents would be when she took Charlie's hand and announced, "Mom, Dad, we have something we need to tell you."

"I close my eyes, Lyddie," Charlie had said Friday night and she couldn't stop hearing him, "and the only thing I can see is your face."

Lydia reversed the boat and opened the throttle wide.

The old motor rooster-tailed to life.

And she leaned forward, unable to breathe again, catching the first open waves. She headed back toward the cedar marina built by a man that everybody in Shadrach wondered if they knew.

CHAPTER THREE

⸻ ❧ ⸻

*S*omeone had left the sprinkler in the schoolyard running all night. On Wednesday morning, a skin of ice coated the grass like shards of glass. Hugging another stack of college-admittance exam booklets to her chest, Lydia walked a broad circle around the ticking, frozen sprinkler and used her derriere to push open the double glass doors to Shadrach High School.

She'd gotten here early enough, she hoped, to avoid staff that might strike up a conversation or ask questions about her long office hours yesterday. Her slip-ons made little rubbery squeaks on the machine-polished floor.

"Whatever you do, don't look up," came a man's voice high overhead that made adrenaline surge through her.

She looked up, her heart in her throat. "Charlie?"

"Hi there."

When the architect had designed renovations to the

school building, the old-timers in town had thought it awful. Now the school had newfangled beams inside, heavy cement blocks, open iron trusses. There sat Charlie and several students on a truss, hanging over her head with three different tool belts wrapped over beams.

"What are you doing?"

"Homecoming decorations," he informed her. "Nibarger decided we were the only ones who knew how to handle a nail gun."

A huge piece of plywood swayed to and fro. Lydia had to step back to see the rounded corners, the silhouette of a monstrous school mascot. In a white dialogue balloon the snake incited GO FIRE-RATTLERS! BURN THE BLAZERS! HOMECOMING 2003. Its fangs jutted at fierce angles from its open serpent jaws.

Lydia watched Charlie for . . . what? Some clue? A tip-off that he might not be what he seemed to be? But there he sat, just the Charlie she loved. Just the Charlie she would spend her life with here in Shadrach. Or so they had both planned, before Shelby Tatum had revealed her terrible story.

Lydia broke off the stare they shared. "I'd better go."

"Yeah," Charlie said to the kids, "I've got a class to get ready for, too. You guys, we have to make sure this thing is secure. Check that end, would you?" They took turns tightening the hooks, crimping the chain. "Who can help again fourth period? Jason, stop waving your hand. You've got a calculus test."

Lydia started toward her office. Behind her, she heard the clatter of ladder rungs sliding, a paintbrush falling to the ground.

"You guys clean up here, okay?"

She heard the thud as his shoes hit the floor.

"Hey. Hey, *Lyddie*." He grabbed her elbow and she spun around. Despite his jovial tone, his eyes hinted of worry. "What did you do all day yesterday? I thought you were going to come by my classroom after sixth period."

"I . . . I had a meeting with a student. It lasted awhile."

The ordinariness of Charlie's greeting, the openness of his smile, made Shelby's claim seem all the more ugly. Uglier than death. *A single man around high school girls.* Air forced itself into her lungs against her will. She toyed with the absurd, impossible thing. *He's been alone for a long time. And if he wanted me . . .*

"I even phoned your uncle's place last night. He said he hadn't seen you."

"He told me."

"Well, then. I wish you had called."

Other schoolteachers began to arrive, the muffled monotones of the inner sanctum coming to life. Every conversation was about someone, undertones, words drifting mysteriously in and out of rooms.

"Is something wrong?" he asked. "Are you having second thoughts? Is that it?"

"*No,*" she said, the one word so vehement that she made him flinch.

"Then why are you looking at me like that, Lyddie?"

"Like what?"

"Like you're seeing somebody you don't know."

"I . . . I'm not doing that, am I?" Then, before he had the chance to dispute her, "I have to get to my office. I've got a lot to do this morning."

The hissing of air brakes came from outside, the safety beeps of a Shadrach Sanitation truck. The garbage truck played D-flat, measured and perfect, as it reversed toward the nearest Dumpster.

I ought to come right out and ask him. I ought to say, "Do you know what Shelby told me?"

He'd think she doubted him. If she asked, he'd think she didn't trust him. There could be no turning back if she went forward with this; the damage would be done.

I don't need reassurances with Charlie. He said himself, I know him better than his own family.

She knew he touched the thin spot on his sideburn when he was perplexed and she knew how it tickled him when she rubbed between his big toe and the next one, and she knew that when he came up after swimming underwater there was always a little pool of water caught in the scoop of his throat.

She knew that cat dander gave him the sniffles. She knew he felt responsible for his parents because he was the youngest out of four. She knew he'd once hit five for five in a Little League baseball tournament and that he had played catcher and his best friend, Jay Lundeen, had played pitcher and that every week they'd changed their signals because the coach from Hollowsville was always trying to figure them out.

She knew the silent, dark-river-eyed look of him whenever he disapproved of something. She knew the sweat smell of him when he'd just come in from running. She knew how handsome he looked dressed in his gray Brooks Brothers suit and his yellow-flecked tie.

Two steps down the school hall, filled with personal despair, and she turned to say with a lowered voice, "Charlie?"

"What?"

"You know a girl named Shelby Tatum?"

"Who?"

"A sophomore. Shelby Tatum."

A beat. Two. "Oh, Shelby. Sure. I've got her third period, don't I?"

"Yeah, you've got her."

He didn't respond as if anything was out of the ordinary.

Lydia stood, fluorescent bulbs giving out a gentle buzz overhead. She had that sort of middle pain that made her feel hollowed out, ready to crumble inward. "What sort of a student is she?"

"Quiet. Good. B student. Why do you ask?"

She watched his face for signs of unease. *Please, no. Please.* She didn't see any. The relief made her dizzy. "She's been talking to me about things, Charlie."

"Oh?" A flicker came, a slight change in his expression. She didn't know what it meant but she saw it.

"Yes."

It might not have even been noticeable. But she'd seen it, although it had passed too quickly for her to analyze. She could have imagined it. She couldn't be sure. And then, the shadow of concern in his eyes, the tightening of the cords in his neck. "Is everything okay with her, Lydia? Is there anything I can do to help?"

He had caught up with her in the hallway. When he touched her shoulder, she longed to grab his fingers and to hold them against her skin, to hold on to the hopeless affection, the curl of pleasure that came whenever Charlie was near.

"No, I don't think so."

Maybe this isn't real. Maybe I didn't see what I thought I saw. Maybe Shelby didn't say what I thought she said. Maybe everything I thought I understood isn't understandable at all.

But what else did Lydia have to believe in besides her own ears and eyes?

She stood still, her clammy palms clamped around the edges of the newsprint booklets, knowing that she had become confident and sure of herself because this man loved her. She ached from holding her mouth steady. "Charlie, she said some things about *you.*"

"About me?"

"Yes."

He looked lost, as if he had no idea what she was talking

about. Then he gave a little smile, as if he had it all figured out. "She said I was the best teacher she had ever had. That she wants to take woodshop every semester from now on until she graduates."

"No. That isn't it."

"Mr. S? Mr. S!" A cluster of girls bounded up in the hall just then, bouncing and eager, a mixture of gawky colt and prima ballerina.

They surrounded Charlie. "Hey," he clapped his hands, not quite as enthusiastic as usual, reluctant to draw his eyes from Lydia's. "What's all the excitement here?"

One girl wore her hair in blonde tufts that resembled the weeds growing from the cracks in the outdoor basketball court. "We want to help with homecoming decorations. If we come out during sixth period, will you let us do something?"

Lydia focused on his left jaw, the inverted heart-shaped fold and shadow of his ear. "I can't do it then," he said. "I have to leave the building during sixth period." He stepped sideways and caught Lydia's gaze. "Because I've bought a fishing boat."

It was something, he'd confided to her, that he'd always dreamed of having. Once, sitting on the edge of Cy Porter's new dock at sundown, their bare feet skimming ribbons in the water, he'd told her he'd had a name picked out for it since he was thirteen.

Charlie's Pride.

"This is it, Lyddie," he started off, grinning at her. "I

43

know maybe it sounds crazy. There are so many other things we—" He stopped. *There are so many other things we're going to need once we get married.* If he'd said too much, it didn't matter. The troupe of girls had already lost interest and disbanded toward their lockers. "They had a sign about it up over at Show Me Kwik Gas," he said. "Somebody dropped this boat, in its trailer, off in the front lawn of Big Tree Baptist. In the middle of the night."

"Charlie," she said, knowing she had to make him listen. "By law, I'm required to report the story Shelby told me."

"Just parked a boat by the front door and drove away. Church folks decided that Jesus or God or somebody must want them to auction it off. They've been taking sealed bids all week down at the Show Me."

Lydia made a small, indeterminate sound. It should have been one of those slightly comic moments, something she could tease him about later, her fiancé purchasing something he said he'd always wanted right before they announced their engagement to everyone they knew.

"Somebody called this morning and said I'd won." He looked like a little boy who'd bought something he shouldn't have. "I've never had a fish finder, either. That came with it."

Before Lydia could stop him, he pitched the keys to his truck to her. "You mind driving me back in the GMC? That trailer isn't too sturdy and I wanted to keep a close eye out the window."

"Charlie—"

"And you know," he said, winking at her, "it isn't just *any* girl that I would trust to drive my truck."

"—did you hear me?"

Just a smile in the hallway, a conversation or two, a distant knowledge of Shelby's family, an adolescent girl who'd seemed a little over friendly, anxious to have a friend.

How could I think I don't trust him? How could I even think?

"You have to understand that they don't ask me to pass judgment. And I'm not. Certainly not about this."

He took one step toward her. "Lydia, what are you talking about?"

"You don't know?" she asked, and then she wanted to smack herself because she'd made it sound like she expected him to.

"No, I don't."

Now that she'd come this far, she did not want to voice the ugly thing. But she forced herself, while his truck keys lay heavy and warm in her hand. "Shelby Tatum. Have you ever touched her, Charlie? Have you done anything wrong?"

"Huh?" He jerked up his chin and frowned at her. "Whadyousay?"

"Has anything inappropriate happened between you and your student, Charlie?" She had never meant to take it this far. She had only meant to feel him out before she went to the principal.

He pinched the bridge of his nose with two fingers and stared at her in disbelief. "Why would you even ask that?"

"Because she says it has."

His body reacted first. He straightened, arched his spine, as if the shock coursed through him like electricity. "What?"

"You heard what I said."

"She's accusing me?"

"Yes."

She could see he wanted to pound something. He wheeled away, slapped a row of lockers, then hung his head. He did a hard, Army-style pushup against the wall.

Slowly, as if it was all he could do to contain his anger, he turned toward her. He stood with his chin raised and his jaw square. He threw words as if he was throwing dirt clods in her direction. "If she told you that, she's lying."

Yes, yes. Oh, yes, I know. Of course I know she is.

"I shouldn't be worried, should I, Lyddie? This isn't going to be a problem, is it? She's just some messed-up kid."

"There are a lot of people who might not think she's messed up at all."

"Well," he asked without missing a beat. "Do you?"

Her chin jerked up. She stared at him.

"Oh, Charlie."

This time he did hit the wall, leaning hard against the flats of his hands. He held the flex as if he could shove all of his anger and frustration into the wall of the school.

Oh please do something better than that, she wanted to beg him. *Say something that will make it easy for me to stop this right here.*

CHAPTER FOUR

*L*ydia eased open the door to Mrs. Brubaker's second-period advanced-algebra class that Wednesday morning. Through the crack she could hear chalk clicking fervently on the blackboard. "In this case—" *Tap tap tap* went the chalk. "—*degree* refers to the largest exponent of the variables in a polynomial. For example, if the largest exponent of the variable is 3, as in Ax-cubed plus Bx-squared plus Cx, the polynomial is of degree 3."

Sunlight blazed in through the windows. Rows of students slumped at haphazard angles in their seats, the full weight of their chins propped on their elbows. Whitney Allen, the captain of the Rattler-Den dance team, focused her complete attention on the ribbon dangling from one hank of her hair. Behind Whitney, Adam Buttars drummed his yellow No. 2 pencil against the open pages of his textbook. With sleight of hand, Cassie Meade slipped a note across the aisle to Will Devine. Will socked it away with a magician's stealth and dexterity.

"There you have it," the teacher said to the chalkboard. "When you have x to the n plus x to the n-minus-1 plus x to the n-minus-2, the equation is of degree n. Any questions about that?" Followed by a dull, unresponsive silence.

Lydia waited a full twenty seconds before she whispered "Knock, knock" and poked her head inside the door. In a hushed voice, "You mind if I interrupt?"

The chalk rolled into the tray. "No problem." Judy Brubaker straightened and dusted off her hands.

"I need to see one of your kids in the counseling office. You mind?"

The algebra teacher pulled open a drawer, took out a stack of peel-off hall passes. "Which one?"

"Shelby Tatum."

"I'm afraid I can't do that." Judy dropped the pad of passes inside the drawer again and Lydia's heart plummeted to her toes. "That one came through as an unexcused absence this morning."

"I see."

"Sorry. No Shelby today."

Lydia hurried back down the hall to the office, her sandals making a rapid *ker-snap ker-snap* on the floor. "We don't have an excused absence for Tatum?" she asked as she passed the first row of metal workstations.

Someone called after her, "Nothing from a parent yet."

Lydia headed straight for the multi-use file cabinet in

Mayhem Central, which is what the teachers called the administration office. She wound her way through five different staff members doing five different things, yanked open the third drawer, and rifled through the queue of green, dog-eared forms.

Tanner.

Tasker.

Tattersall.

Ah, there she was. *Tatum*, S. Lydia seized the paper from its place and squired the St. Clair County School District Emergency Information Form back to her quiet cubicle, reading the entire time.

Social security number, birth date, insurance policy. Mother or guardian's name: *Tamara Tatum Olin, who resides at 913 Sweetwater Court, Shadrach*. Physician: *Dr. Stanley Lerch, with his clinic in Osceola*. In case of emergency contact: *Mr. Milburn Woodruff, same address, different number*. Relationship to student: *grandfather*. Yes, the box was checked, my child may have Tylenol and topical first-aid preparation. No, my child does not have any known allergies. Yes, my child may participate in field trips.

There were no notes saying: *Yes, this child can exaggerate. Yes, this girl often tells stories for attention. Yes, she sometimes fibs and causes problems.*

Lydia dragged her telephone across her desk, punched a button for an open line and dialed the establishment listed as mother's workplace.

"Shadrach Land Title," a girl answered like she was sing-ing a Branson country song. "You can't *lien* on us."

"Tamara Olin, please."

"Just a moment, please."

What has happened at your house, Mrs. Olin? Why isn't your daughter in my office today?

A quiet whirring came, and the line was connected. Someone else picked it up, asked, "You looking for Tammy?"

"Yes."

"She isn't in, I'm afraid. Some sort of family emergency or something."

The adrenaline buzz began in Lydia's ears again, heavy and unnavigable, stealing her senses.

"Perhaps someone else in the office can help you."

"No . . . I mean, well, this is a personal call."

"She may be at home. You might want to try her there."

"I will."

Lydia dialed a second string of digits and waited, her hand gripping the earpiece as if everything depended on it; if she clasped the receiver hard enough against her head, Shelby might answer the phone.

I didn't know the name you were going to give me was Charlie's.

After all I coaxed you to say, you have to find someone else to do this for you. I can't get tied up in this, do you understand?

The answering machine picked up and all the breath

went out of her. She sat through a garbled message and a long series of beeps before she finally admitted that no one would be answering at the house.

Where could they be, if Shelby was sick? If she was trying to change a lie? Or if she had broken down, trying to make them hear her?

The fourth period bell rang. From outside the counseling office, conversation spilled in. "At senior night there were seven of them, a couple of big girls that are coming up, two sophomores, and one little point guard. But I don't—"

The conversation faded down the hall.

Oh, Father. How do I know what to believe?

On Lydia's desk sat a half-empty jar of candy Kisses. She dug for one, took it out and twisted, twisted the wrapper until the foil fell to pieces between her fingers.

Of course, I believe Charlie. I'm in love with Charlie.

With painful care, she set the tear-shaped chocolate on her desk. She stared at it until it began to swim before her eyes.

∽

IN MAYHEM CENTRAL, the copier was acting up. Patrice Saunders stood leafing through the Xerox instruction booklet while some unknown staff member—unrecognizable from the body parts that protruded from the midsection of the machine—yanked wads of paper from its path of rubber rollers. Some sophomore with a bloody rag under his nose stood dripping on the floor while the secretary, Marie Jones, went in search of Mo. At Marie's station, the telephone was ringing and three holding lines flashed off and on at the same time.

Lydia returned the Tatum form to its place. As she did, she was the first to notice a woman standing at the counter, her fingers in a prim, tight weave, leaning on her elbows.

When Lydia turned back to her files, the woman rang the bell for help. Lydia glanced over a shoulder toward Marie's chair, a little disgruntled because no one else would step up. "Hello," the woman said to Lydia's shoulder blades, her voice as thin as a ribbon. "I just need to pick up my daughter's homework. I'm Tamara Olin."

The metal drawer trundled all the way open of its own accord. Lydia got ahold of the handle and clanged it shut. "You're Shelby Tatum's mother?"

In a warm, embarrassed voice the woman said, "I know I should have called earlier to excuse her."

"We've been trying to reach you all day."

"Oh, you know." The woman waved it away as if she was shooing a fly. "It's been one of those crazy mornings."

Just then, several cheerleaders came charging in. One of the most anticipated events for Shadrach homecoming was the annual powder-puff football game. In a turn of roles each year, the eleventh- and twelfth-grade girls played against each other in a gridiron match-up while the boys rooted them on from the sidelines. This year a group of senior boys had offered to dress up as cheerleaders and do stunts. The kids had been whispering about it for weeks.

The girls were excited. "Is Kevin here yet? They said they were sending somebody from yearbook."

"Why is somebody from yearbook coming?" Lydia asked.

"Didn't you hear?" At last, Marie returned with Mo and a first-aid bag in tow. "L.R. caught wind that the boys have decided to dress up in skirts. He's making all of them come in today to have their outfits approved."

"Right now?"

"He won't let them dress that way unless the school board says yes."

"Do you have homework for Shelby Tatum?" Lydia asked Marie.

"Right here." The wire baskets were stacked as high as a St. Louis skyscraper. Marie pointed to the top tier. "If anybody put stuff together for her, it would be there."

Lydia thumbed through. Sure enough, she found a folder with Shelby's name scribbled on it. She opened to the first page and saw that Mrs. Brubaker had slipped a note and an assignment inside. Mr. Newkirk had added a reading list for French II. Lydia closed it, handed it over.

But Mrs. Olin didn't quite get a grip on the folder. Papers fell out and scattered everywhere. "Oh, so sorry." Mrs. Olin shook her head in frustration and began scraping everything across the counter toward her. "I'll get this."

Lydia remembered her grandma saying once, "There's no reason having a double-duck fit, saying things you don't want to say. A conversation doesn't please you, you just don't have it." She touched the strap of the woman's wrist-watch; there was a long, poignant meeting of eyes.

"I'd like to discuss something with you."

The woman's eyes moved to the countertop again. "Oh, sorry I dropped all of this." She finally had the papers organized, almost in a stack. That's when Lydia noticed the top corner of one page sticking out, a note with Shelby's name on it, scribbled in Charlie's hasty, heavy hand.

"I just—" Lydia reached for it.

"Oh, no. No." Tamara Olin picked Shelby's assignments up and tamped them on the counter. "I'm the one who scattered these all over the place." Unceremoniously, she slid them back inside the folder for safekeeping and tucked the folder under one arm.

"If I could just—" Lydia's fingers stopped in midair. The familiar shape and form of Charlie's script, the slanted, slender forcefulness of the *S*, the *h* a pointed tent as distinct and identifiable as a thumbprint.

Oh my word, Charlie. What are you doing?

Just then the door flung open; the hooting and catcalls rang out. In traipsed an entire roster of senior boys, raucous and free in their status—*It's almost over, we've almost survived Shadrach and are escaping soon to taste the rest of the world*—ready to display their outrageous attire to L. R. Nibarger, the principal.

Nibarger had put the word out that in no uncertain terms were the actions of the students to detract from, as he put it, "the diligent pride and upstanding character of those who have attended this institution before us, and the strong sensibilities of the community of Shadrach that has given us so much support over the decades." These boys looked to be doing everything they could to push the envelope. Will Devine entered carrying his aunt's Hawaiian muumuu. Ian McNeil had his outfit—an embroidered peasant blouse that, Patrice Saunders had told them, came from Natalie Stokes's rummage sale—on a hanger in a plastic bag from Run O' The Mill Dry Cleaners.

Yearbook photographer Kevin Champa crouched low with a Pentax screwed to his eye. A burst of light from the camera's flash, and Lydia knew she couldn't let Tamara go without mentioning something about Shelby. One carefully worded phrase. *Something.*

"I talked to Shelby just yesterday."

You did? she expected Tamara would say. Or, *Oh yes, she told me.*

But, "I've *wanted* her to talk to you," the woman said, smiling, and Lydia's throat closed with disbelief. "I've been *encouraging* her."

"You have?"

"Of course I have. She's going to have so many opportunities when the time comes. If Missouri and Ole Miss both offer her the scholarships we're expecting, I don't know what she's going to do."

"I wasn't—"

"If it wasn't against the rules, she would already have

been hearing from coaches by now. She's going to have a very difficult—"

"Okay, Leavitt." Nibarger made a small notation on an index card he'd pulled from his rear pocket. "The skirt is fine."

"This conversation wasn't about college. It was a little more serious than that." Lydia moved a vase of wilted mums an inch to the left; it had been sitting there in the same spot for at least two weeks. "Perhaps we should sit down somewhere. Maybe we could visit about this."

"Visit about what? Did she say she has some kind of problem? Shelby doesn't have any problems." The words suddenly high-pitched and tumbling. "And besides, you know how it is. You can't always believe everything a teenager says. You know how teenage girls are sometimes." A careful shrug. "You know you can't take adolescent drama—"

"No." Nibarger gestured wildly toward Tommy Ballard as the entire counseling staff, excluding Lydia Porter, applauded. "No, not that. You may not wear a coconut brassiere." He pronounced it as if the very word was distasteful to him. Bra-*zeeeer*. He held out his hand. "In fact, why don't I just confiscate that right now?"

Tommy handed it over with obvious pride, two halves of coconut shell bound at strategic junctures with twine.

Strange how humans are, Lydia thought. When Mrs. Olin said not to take Shelby seriously, Lydia began to take her even more so.

"Do you talk to your daughter, Mrs. Olin?"

"Oh, we talk all the time. We're very close, especially since I married Tom. She's so happy now." The woman was passionate in her sincerity. "When I was married to Shelby's father, our lives were insane. He spent money like it was growing on trees. Do you know that his mother wanted to pick the names of our children?" Tamara ran on and on. "Since I met Tom, I don't think I could ever have another life. Gosh, Tom just loves Shelby. Like his own daughter, he says. He wouldn't miss a soccer game if his life depended on it."

It was an old counseling joke and it popped right into Lydia's head. *Denial,* counselors always laughed. *It ain't just a river in Egypt.* This woman rattled on and on as if someone had dropped a quarter in her slot.

"Last Mother's Day, she made me certificates. Good for one foot rub before you go to bed. Good for one manicure. Good for one car wash. Now who would have known how she'd come up with something like that? She helps with vacation Bible school at Big Tree, and those kids sit in her lap; they tumble all over her like puppies. Drives her crazy but don't let her convince you she doesn't like it. Shelby's a drama queen sometimes, but you couldn't ask for better. I tell you, she's one person I know who's got the world by the tail."

Sam Leavitt joined them then, pulling his mother's skirt around his pelvis, working it off past the basketball shorts that he wore underneath.

"Hey, Miss P. Hey, Missus Olin, where's Shelby? I ordered her this big red flower for homecoming and I've got to tell her to find something to wear that'll match it."

Maybe the note Lydia had seen, with Shelby's name scrawled in Charlie's handwriting, had been only a class assignment. Maybe it was only that. Lydia's heart seemed to lift up out of itself with the indecision, as if it was weightless, pushing up against her chest.

Could this woman's house be on fire and she doesn't see it?

Could it be the stepfather maybe? *Tom, she'd said. Gosh, Tom just loves Shelby. Like his own daughter, he says.*

If she won't listen to me, she isn't listening to Shelby.

Nobody's listening to Shelby. Not even me.

CHAPTER FIVE

ydia walked the hallway back to her office in a daze during fifth period, her peripheral vision spinning gray around her. In a building she knew so well that she could have found her way blindfolded, she made a wrong turn up A-hall.

She backtracked, angry at herself for being so distracted. She found Carol Hawkes, the other guidance counselor, on the opposite side of the college catalog bookshelves. "Carol? Can I talk to you for a minute?"

"Sure."

"I need help."

"So, what else is new?" But Carol's voice sobered when Lydia didn't laugh. "Help with something professional? You'd better tell me."

So much going on in her heart, and Lydia knew she had to remain sophisticated about this. "A student came into my office late yesterday and she . . ." This wasn't the first time something had happened like this, even in Shadrach. She knew what to do. She had to present the idea as formally and as professionally as if the perpetrator wasn't someone she cared about.

"What?"

"This student told me that she has been sexually abused by someone."

Carol laid down the college catalog she'd been riffling through.

"This someone, Carol. It's . . . it's somebody in the *school*."

"Well, of course she is. The student—"

"No," Lydia said pointedly. "That isn't what I mean. Not only the student."

"What?" And then, "Oh, my word." The conversation stopped there, hung between them like a pendulum ready to swing.

"I need you to help me."

"Well, of course I will. I'll do anything. But—"

This idea had been growing in Lydia's mind ever since she'd heard Tamara Olin speaking about her family. Like an animal caught in a snare, it was impossible for her to move one way or another. "Will you do it for me, Carol?"

Carol stared at her. "What?"

"Will you make the report to Nibarger?"

Carol shook her head. "Don't ask me to do that. You

know how important it is for you to be there. You're the one required by the district to do it."

"I could help you with the paperwork. I just . . . you could tell him that it's somebody I don't—"

"You remember what happened in the Richard Janke case. Those teachers were charged with negligence because they didn't go to the state. You're the one they'll want when the Department of Health and Human Services comes along. There will be plainclothesmen, too, and they're going to have all their questions."

"Does it matter who reports it as long as it gets reported? You could do it, Carol. It would be so simple."

"They'll want specifics of what she said. Uncontaminated evidence from the *student*. There isn't anybody who can do that now except for you."

No, Father. I can't do this. Please.

"You're the one she trusted to talk to in the first place. You've done it before, and the police are going to expect it from you again, Lydia. You've got to remind her that she's safe. Encourage her."

"Carol, if you'd consider it—"

"I won't consider it. I don't know why you're even asking."

Charlie pressing her against him, drawing her close until her spine curved against the shape of him like the curve of a barrel stave.

Charlie, whose love polished her life the way his hands polished jack-oak and hickory—honing, refining, coaxing out the shine.

All this time, and Carol must have been studying the play of emotions on her face. "This person the girl is accusing, Lydia. You're acting as if it is one of our *friends*."

Lydia didn't say anything else. Now *there* was a stupid statement, and they both knew it.

"It is, isn't it?" Carol asked.

Everybody was friends with everybody else in the halls of Shadrach High, especially since they'd all settled down about Charlie Stains moving home.

༅

LYDIA WAS TRAPPED. Caught fast. As obligated to care for Shelby as she was to care for Charlie. Add to that, she hadn't found a way to get out of driving with him to pick up his newly purchased boat.

It isn't just any girl I would trust to drive my truck, he'd said.

And so, with a heavy heart, she didn't back out of her promise.

Big Tree Baptist Church, perhaps the most visible and noted landmark in St. Clair County, sat like a white wedding-cake top along the ridge of Elbow Knob.

Out by the road, down the hill a little ways, the sign said VICTORY BAPTIST CHURCH. But the summer Addy Michael had gotten saved, she'd started bringing her three rambunctious boys along. Her youngest one—three-year-old Henry—couldn't say "Victory" very well. *Oh, big tree in Je-sus, my savior forever,* Henry would sing at the top of his lungs. *He sought me and bought me with his redeeming blo-oo-od.*

"Well, that works," the pastor's wife, Emma, had said. "Jesus died on the cross, and it was a big tree." That, plus all those white oaks and old cedars, honey locusts and chestnuts that God made to blanket Shadrach's hardwood slopes, had sealed it. No matter what the sign said out front, the place had been known as Big Tree Baptist ever since.

When Lydia drove into the church parking lot in Charlie's truck, they only had thirty minutes or so to pick up his auction boat.

The slim craft sat on the lawn out front, gleaming like a missile in its trailer, tipped stern-down and prow-up. It looked like a bullfrog ready to leap.

"I'll go in and pay them," he said, his voice grim after their earlier conversation. Then, pointedly: "I wouldn't want anyone to think I'm getting away with something."

Lydia wasn't listening to him. She sat with her fingers in a light curl around the wheel, touching the stitched leather as if to remind herself that it was there, the same way she touched the possibility that Shelby could be telling the truth.

His truck door creaked as he threw it open.

She didn't want to climb out and follow him. She wanted to stay inside his truck holding her breath. She wanted this precipice, this falling-off place in her heart, to go away. She wanted everything to stay the same.

Charlie didn't look back at her. He slid out and walked to the boat. He ran his hand along the resin, searching for scratches and chips near the rivets. He found several. Every time he found one he stopped, rubbed hard with his thumb, trying to rub away the damage.

"I had such big plans," he said, his voice brimming with bitterness. "I was going to take your dad out, show him the way we sail in Missouri. Forget the wind. I was going to let a big-mouthed bass take hold and pull us along."

"My father already knows how to do that. Uncle Cy taught him." Reluctantly, Lydia edged out of the seat and slid past the running boards to the ground. "Charlie—"

"Was looking forward to getting the name painted on the boat." He talked as if his whole life had ended, now that he understood what Shelby was accusing him of. "Was going to get the lettering done in blue and gold, by a professional at Shadrach Signs."

"Charlie—" She came up behind him, her arms at her sides, her mouth feeling like she'd swallowed a cotton boll. "What did you do with your kids today?"

He was traipsing around the bow of the vessel he'd named *Charlie's Pride*, his footsteps digging deep into the gravel. "I couldn't wait to moor her at the new dock at Viney Creek. The new *Porter* dock." He turned, stopped. It must have taken that long for her question to sink in. "What do you mean, what did I do with my kids?"

"In class."

He shrugged, furrowed his brows at her. "What we always do in class. Build things."

She asked this next thing as lightly as a butterfly descends and settles, barely landing, fluttering away again. She hated herself for checking up on him this way. She couldn't stop thinking about the note to Shelby she'd caught a glimpse of. "Any homework this week?"

"No." A frown. "Why?"

"Do you ever assign any homework when the kids miss class?"

Say yes, Charlie. Yes. Say that, just for Shelby, you sent something today.

"When we study joinery. I'll assign homework for everybody then. They'll go out to search for basic joints."

"That's the only time you'd send an assignment home? Joinery?"

"Tongue and groove joints. Bevel joints. Dovetails and miters and lap joints. They'll drive everyone crazy, looking. We're doing finishes now. Smoothing with sandpaper and steel wool. Applying waxes, oils, stains—"

He broke off his train of thought suddenly and stared down at her. "What are you doing? Checking up on me or something? You still want to know if I've had anything to do with that girl?"

"Did you send something home in Shelby Tatum's homework packet today?"

He met her intent scrutiny head on, his face a shield. "No."

She needed to escape. The afternoon sun tinted everything around her a translucent saffron—the tree limbs, the jagged rocks along the sidewalk, the steeple that pierced the sky like a radiant awl. Uncle Cy had said once that he felt the golden presence of something here, as real as when he watched the sun rise and the blue haze sink toward the water like a coverlet, down at the Brownbranch.

"Lydia? Don't you believe me?"

"I'll take your check in, if you'd like. You can stay out here and fondle your new boat." *Fondle.* Now why had she used such a word as that? "I need to get away."

He said nothing to her. He reached for his blank checks and tore one across its perforation with an angry, brittle sound.

"You can't act like what Shelby's saying doesn't matter."

For a long moment he just stood with that bruised expression in his eyes. And she stared up, past him, as if directions for what to do next were printed beside the steeple in the sky.

"I wanted to talk to her, Lydia," he said in the mangled voice of someone having a nightmare. "I wrote her that note to see if we could discuss this, if we could work out what's going on. Please don't judge me until I've had a chance to do that."

She took Charlie's check from him. "I'm not judging," she whispered, closing her eyes because she couldn't look at him anymore, "but I can't let you have access to her. I won't let you talk to her or see her again." In the silence between them, the contention began to grow, something tense and sullen and explosive. "I told her I would protect her. I don't know what else I'm supposed to do."

∽

WHEN LYDIA STEPPED through the heavy front door, the inside of Big Tree Baptist smelled faintly musty, like carnations and crisp paper and ginger windmill cookies. As she entered the narrow foyer with Charlie's check in hand, she entered the place where she had first come to believe that she deserved to be loved. Aunt Donna, Uncle Cy's wife-before-Jane, had brought her here every summer when she'd come to visit. She remembered pie suppers and Layne Shanholtz standing behind the microphone and singing "When We All Get to Heaven," his voice turned up so loud on the speakers that it sounded like the woofers might burst. She wondered sometimes, out of all the kids she had met loitering in the kitchen, if one of them—even then—might have been Charlie Stains. There had never been time, during those visiting summers, to know everyone's name.

Although her own parents had never taken her to church, Aunt Donna had brought her and, in this place, Lydia had come to believe things always easy for a child to believe. And after she had graduated college, after she had accepted her teaching position and had moved to Shadrach full time, Lydia still came.

She detoured now and stepped into the sanctuary. At the front of the little church, a hickory altar stood gleaming with furniture oil. Light streamed upon it in rays of gold, red, and blue from the pattern in the stained-glass window above it. How strange that, when Charlie had bought a boat, it would have to be picked up here.

At that moment she heard a noise down the hall. A scuffling on the carpet, as if someone might be dancing.

Then, *blam.* Something hard hit the wall.

She wasn't alone in the building. Lydia's first fear was that someone might have overheard her conversation with Charlie outside. She stood listening, motionless, wondering if the sound would come again.

It did.

Charlie's check for the boat was still crammed inside her pocket. Lydia began to make her way along the wall toward the sound. She followed the noise until she came to a door that opened like the barn door on *Mr. Ed*, separated into halves, the bottom latched tight, the top swinging open an inch or two.

AGES 3 AND 4 read a metal placard that had been screwed into the drywall. Below that, in a red Magic Marker: *Please pick up your child immediately following the service. No child will be allowed to leave without a parent.*

She tried the knob. Once upon a time, this had been where the smell of the cookies had come from. The hinges squeaked and the rest of the door began to swing wide. Suddenly, in an odd moment of providence, even before the door opened far enough for her to see, Lydia knew exactly who would be standing on the other side.

Shelby.

And sure enough, there she was, alone in the preschool Sunday school room, sidestepping her soccer ball, foot working it forward and back, as if the ball, the way she shot it, the way it moved, absorbed all of her attention. Shelby zigzagged the ball right, left, right, left, until she shot, *bam*, through a goal she'd set up through two miniature Sunday school chairs.

"So this is what you do when you skip school? You come here instead?"

The ball rebounded and Shelby grabbed it, tucked it against her right hipbone. She cocked her knee, a motion that belied the unease in her eyes. "Sometimes," she said, her voice more broody than Lydia had ever heard it before.

"What are you doing here?"

"I could ask the same question about you."

Shelby balanced the ball—HAND-SEWN BUTYL BLADDER it said—then spun it back and forth between both hands. She surveyed Lydia with suspicion. "Who said I was skipping school?"

"A lucky guess, I suppose." Lydia shrugged. "Your mother came to pick up your homework. Does she know where you've been all day?"

A hard and fragile laugh, sounding as if she was about to break. "Why would she know where I am? I don't fit into her perfect little world." Then, with gusto, "I don't fit into anybody's world but my own."

Lydia looked around for a place to sit. She decided if she tried to fit into one of those nursery-school chairs, she might never make it out again.

69

The resentment in Shelby's voice eased, but only a little. "Were you trying to find me today?"

"Yes." Lydia had no reason to lie.

"Why?"

"Why do you think? I was worried about you."

"Well, you don't have to worry about me anymore. I don't need anything from anybody. Least of all *you*." They sized each other up across the room. "You said you'd help me. But you didn't do anything."

"You didn't come to school today."

"Yeah, and I guess you'd know why." A suspicious thump of shoes on the carpet. A suspicious gleam of disenchantment in her eyes. Shelby dropped the soccer ball on the floor again, began to dribble it frontward with slight touches of her feet.

"Have you told anyone about this but me?"

"What does it matter? Nobody cares."

"Did you try to tell your mom?"

All of her focus on the ball, a wild, wayward-shaking "no" of the bunched hair.

"Why, Shelby?"

Everything in this playroom was on a Lilliputian scale—chairs so simple and small they might have come straight out of a nursery rhyme, tabletops on square legs so short they abutted a grown person's shins. A row of crumpled little stained-glass windows, fashioned from flecks of crayon ironed between wax paper, lined one wall.

Shelby evaded that question. She aimed the soccer ball,

shot it in frustration, *bam* against the wall. "I should have known better than to ask anybody for anything. I've been taking care of myself for a long time now. Guess I'll just have to keep on doing things on my own."

The shot rebounded against Lydia's calf. She grabbed it with both hands.

"Guess I'll just make better and better grades," Shelby said. "Guess I'll just beat the pants off of every goalie who tries to stop me."

Lydia held the ball, made Shelby look at her, before she bounced it back. "You're going to break a hole through the drywall, you keep hitting it with the ball like that."

"The way you poked around and made me talk to you. I thought you'd be"—Shelby caught the ball beneath the weight of one foot, kicked again, shanked it—*"different."*

"Shelby, you don't have to take care of yourself anymore. People are going to listen."

"I did something to make it happen, didn't I? I'm the one who could have made it all go away."

Those words hit Lydia like a fist. They grabbed hold, turned within her, invoked something sinister there. A memory of her own school years; a memory she'd always tried to escape, a situation that she thought she had prayed about and taken to the Lord a long time ago. *Her own sophomore year, and Mr. Buckholtz.*

She wanted to shake Shelby's shoulders, but she couldn't. "No. Listen to me. You didn't *do* anything."

"I must have wanted it or I would have stopped it somehow. I'm thinking maybe I'm the one to blame."

"Don't you ever think that, young lady." Shelby's words made Lydia panic. "You have enough information to know that if something like this happened to you, then what happened to you is wrong."

"It's my fault. Everybody will know that."

If I do nothing else, I can still set this young girl straight about blaming herself.

"You mustn't think that. You mustn't go there, Shelby." Her voice sounded wise and fierce. All these possibilities and Lydia couldn't let go of her own heart. And when she thought back to it later, she could never be sure why she'd jumped to this next declaration so quickly. "He's outside this place right now, you know," she said, in part because she wanted to warn and protect Shelby, in part because she wanted to shock Shelby enough to try to see where she stood.

"He's . . . who?"

"Mr. Stains. He's outside the church right now."

Shelby's face blanched. Her expression changed in an instant from hostility to fear. She caught the soccer ball, held it against her like it was the only thing in the world she knew how to hold on to.

"Does he know I'm in here?"

For months Lydia would remember the sight of Shelby's small hands clutching the polygons of the ball. Nubby nails peeling and innocent, fingers pale as doves, Sam Leavitt's dainty promise ring still too big, listing sadly to one side.

Those eyes, telling Lydia everything that she'd been struggling not to hear.

"I should have been able to make it stop, don't you think? I should have been able to do something and I didn't."

"Shelby." All this time, Lydia had been afraid to touch her. In frustration she gripped the girl's shoulders, holding her there so she couldn't turn away. "Stop believing that about yourself. Stop believing that you controlled it. Stop believing that you're not worth protecting, that you don't deserve to be taken care of, because you *are* and you *do*."

Shelby lowered herself into one of those midget chairs, looking haunted, her knees raftered up to her shoulders, parts of her folded frame hanging off the tiny seat.

"Stop believing that anything about this is your fault."

"I used to go to Sunday school in this room once," Shelby whispered, her voice ravaged. "I used to come here and sit just like this and listen to them say that God could do anything. They still tell little kids that these days, you know? I've heard them."

No, no, Lydia wanted to plead with her. *Don't talk about God right now. Don't do it. Because that's the last place I want to go.*

Like a drone of death, the thought poured into her. *The Lord gives and the Lord takes away.*

The room was a lonely one for all its bright colors and its scribbled drawings, the Little Tyke slide and the wooden play stove in the corner. A lonely place, Lydia saw, for a teenager whose childhood was gone.

A childhood that she claimed had been taken away by Charlie. It always came back to that.

Charlie.

He loves me, she'd remember at odd moments during the day. After which she'd walk a little taller, be a little more honest with people, notice more of them glancing up and smiling her way.

Shelby's body was jammed into a fetal position on the tiny chair, her elbows folded like a willowy bird trying to deflect something with its wings. Kids who'd been hurt the worst, Lydia had known for a long time, could be the most perceptive.

"You don't want to report it, do you?" Shelby's eyes pleading with her even as they accused.

Lydia had let go of the girl's shoulders when Shelby sat. Now she stooped to the girl's level, took the ball, set it on the floor. She gripped Shelby's hands between her own.

"Maybe not," she said with great determination in her voice. "But it doesn't really matter what I want."

CHAPTER SIX

*ydia found Charlie on the Big Tree lawn organizing things in his boat.

He worked with dark determination, his arms up to his elbows in the hull, his expression set as hard as granite. He didn't look her way the entire time he shoved things around.

He stacked and secured two square lifejackets, one on top of the other, like a mason laying two slabs of stone. He thrust the dented first-aid box into a corner beneath the seat. He scraped the empty gas tank toward the outboard with a screech that made her flinch and created a new scratch along the keel.

"Charlie," she said, doing her best to keep her voice even. "Don't."

"What do you mean, don't? I'm just balancing the weight." With angry relish, he thumped three coiled rope loops inside the bow. He crisscrossed the blue-and-yellow oars in the middle, blades forward, poles aft, and began to batten them down. "What took you so long in there?"

She crossed her arms over her bosom the same way the oars were crossed in the boat. "I was . . . looking around." She cringed, having to lie to him. Here they were, talking about trust, and she didn't want him to know she had found Shelby inside.

He jerked the bungee cord as if he were yanking tight the cinch strap of a saddle horse.

A cluster of pecans lay rotting on the grass. Lydia stepped on them one by one, liking the sharp crunches they made underfoot.

Charlie angled out the two-stroke spark-ignition engine for travel; it poked from the stern like a stinger. "How long can it take to hand somebody a check, anyway?"

Lydia uncrossed her arms. She'd forgotten about that altogether. She stuck her hand in her pocket and felt the check there, still crumpled. She pulled it out.

Charlie stared at it. "You didn't give it to them?"

"No."

He must have backed up the truck while she was inside. Alone he had maneuvered it ball-hitch to fender. They were ready to go. "Lyddie, my next class starts in five minutes. What were you *doing?*"

She reacted like a cornered animal. She rounded on him. "I was in the church, okay? Maybe I wanted to pray. Maybe

there are other things going on today that are more important than this secondhand scrap of a boat."

His hands stilled at that. He regarded her with sad, desperate eyes. He didn't open the door. "You think she could
be telling the truth, don't you?"

Of all the questions she'd thought he might ask, she had
least expected this one. She came around the huge fender
toward him. "Charlie, you have to try and understand this.
It doesn't matter what she's telling me. I think I can do my
job without having to be on one side or the other."

"You may think that, Lydia, but you're wrong. Everybody's going to come down on one side of the fence or the
other with this."

"Charlie," she whispered. "I'm on your side. That's what
side of the fence I'm on."

"She's making you doubt me."

"No . . . no no no no. I don't have any doubts. Not about
you."

"It hasn't been twenty-four hours. You're going to Nibarger when we get back, aren't you?"

It hurt worse than hurt itself, like a sudden plunge into
ice water, having to tell him this way. "Yes." Her voice
came so softly, it might have been the breeze mingling
with the leaves. "I am."

They stood with the truck between them, her hand
gritty with dust from the hood where she steadied herself,
his hand on the handle as if he was ready to climb in.

"I want you to do it," he said, resolute. "If you are right

about how important this is, then go ahead. There's no sense you having to be a shield for me."

"I'm not doing that, Charlie. I—" These words opened something new, something she hadn't yet seen in herself.

She wanted to protect him.

All this and she'd *wanted* to be a buffer for him. All this and, while she ached at the choice, she had been thinking she would be the one to choose.

"It's Shelby," Lydia said. "If I turn away from this, I don't know what will happen to her. Don't you see?"

And, suddenly, suddenly, after he'd been almost naïve about the situation earlier, it frightened her that he jumped to this next prediction with such ease. "It's always the kids who come out ahead. It's never the adults who win."

"If you're innocent, you can prove it."

Oh Charlie, Charlie, and in the sun she could see the nick to the left of his chin where he'd shaved wrong and the spike of his cowlick and the two pieces of hair that fell to the aft no matter how many times he combed them the other way.

"It's too late for that already, isn't it?" he said. "In cases like this, the damage is done the moment a word is spoken. After that, parents have a niggling doubt. They never want their sons or daughters in your classes again."

"People *know* you here, Charlie."

"The schools don't want to risk it. And, whoosh, just like that, a teacher is gone."

Only three days ago they'd squatted on their haunches

together at the edge of the dock, the wood still smooth and heavy green and smelling of cedar sap. Their favorite meeting spot, to watch the morning come into the patterns on the lake, like light comes into the facets of a diamond, magnified, multiplied.

Put your hand in the water, Lyddie.

Why?

Sh-hhh. Don't ask. Quick, or you'll miss.

Miss what?

Do you trust me? You'll see.

Let me put my coffee mug down.

Slow. Don't move anything you don't have to move. I'll help you. That's a girl. Now.

His breathing warm on her ear, his chest full length and hard against her back. His arm curved around her as if they were stepping off into a dance, as if he wanted to hold her and set her free all at the same time.

Now, your other hand.

Both of them? You're going to make me fall in.

Sh-hhh.

What?

Here.

He took her second hand himself and placed it inches beside the first one. With his hands cupped around hers in the water, they'd waited, motionless, his chin resting on her shoulder, until he said, *Now. NOW!* and they came up with a brilliant yellow fish, flipping and curling between her hands, as round and as small as her palm. His chin, moving against her shoulder blade. The fish, so beautiful, its heaving yellow middle reflecting glimpses of opal.

It's a sun perch. Brim.

She'd watched as he released it and it side-splashed, then curved its way deep into the water until she couldn't see it anymore. He had entranced her.

Do it again, she breathed. Then, after a long silence, staring down into the lake, *Oh, do it again.*

What do you want me to catch this time, Lyddie?

A bass. Try a big-mouthed bass.

You're crazy. You know there's some things that are easier to catch than others.

The Loch Ness monster, then. Try to catch that. We'd be rich. We'd be famous. With wet fishy hands, she turned into him and grabbed his face. For one frightening moment they lost their balance and she thought that, yes, they were both going to topple into the Brownbranch. But he captured her as they teetered and pulled her against him, rocking his face against her wet palms as he engulfed her with his big arms, both of them laughing.

Then he had caught her wrists inside his hands and the laughter faded, replaced by a serious longing in his eyes that asked much of her. A deep-seated kiss that she almost couldn't bear.

Three mornings ago, and it had been the last time they had touched, the last time they had kissed.

In a loving impulse, Lydia wanted to touch him now. She hungered to remember the planes of his jaw beneath her fingers, wanted the reassurance of his hauling her against his muscle and bone. She needed to hear him say, "It's all right, all right now, Lyddie."

But it wasn't all right.

He backed away from her.

"Just get in the truck, Lydia. We have to get to the school."

"I thought you wanted me to drive."

"Not anymore I don't."

She tried to pray but nothing would come. *Oh, Father.*

The trees screamed out to her in the churchyard. How could you think he would still want you after you've let her accuse him? You fool. You fool. You fool.

Lydia climbed into her side of the truck and slammed the door.

Charlie mounted on his side and yanked the rearview mirror so he could see the boat.

She tucked her knees up with a sullen thump of feet on his dashboard. As if she could make herself invisible, she slouched as low as she could go.

Charlie winched his seatbelt across his pelvis with the same zealous fervor as he would hoist a battle flag. He jerked the gearshift from neutral into first and gave it too much gas. The truck leapt forward.

"There's one thing I know," she told him fiercely as the trailer rattled over the gravel behind them. "Only one thing I know about this. Maybe this isn't the right thing to do,

Charlie," she said, looking down. "But I know it isn't the wrong thing, either."

Charlie didn't reply. His attention stayed on the boat in the rearview mirror.

Charlie's Pride, she wanted to say about that boat, *dragging along behind us.*

He didn't speak at all until they'd gotten clear to the corner of Sassafras and Montgomery and pulled up short by the one traffic signal in town. She stared at the prisms in the stoplight, thinking it looked like an insect eye.

"This boat may be secondhand but it isn't a scrap," he said to the red light. "I've waited my whole life for this."

I have, too, she wanted to say. *Oh me, too.*

CHAPTER SEVEN

ydia lifted her fist to knock on the principal's door. But, for long seconds, she couldn't do it. Cradled inside the crook of one elbow, she carried her report, one manila folder containing three pages that weighed almost nothing.

Three pages.

And they might as well have been a load of bricks for the weight they cast on her heart. This, this was low ground.

She saw the door-handle turn and heard the muted squeak of hinges. Before she could jump out of the way, the door swung toward her. She caught it with her hand to keep it from hitting her shoulder, and there stood L. R. Nibarger, principal, staring down at her, obviously startled.

"Lydia."

"Oh," she said, trying to recover. "I was just coming to talk to you."

"Well, you surprised me."

"Got a minute?"

He checked his watch, stepped backward into his office. He motioned her in. "Well, for you, I certainly do."

"Thank you."

But she didn't move inside yet, not toward him or the desk or the chair. She hadn't been ready. But every guidance counselor had to be ready for something like this when it came. Nibarger sat on the edge of a worktable and waited for her, curiosity sharpening the features on his face. She switched the manila folder from her left hand to her right and finally stepped forward. She offered no further explanation as she slid it toward him.

"What is this?" he asked.

"I think you'd better have a look."

As he read, Lydia stared down at the dark ink, the careful block lettering, her own meticulous writing. And as she did, she wished she could be anywhere but here—out with the autumn-evening leaf smells or sniffing the damp red earth that her Uncle Cy had taught her to love or hearing the lap of water as it licked at the lakeshore. Nibarger was biting his bottom lip so hard it had turned white as he read, his eyes tracking left to right along the page, Lydia's heart moving with his eyes, wishing that she'd never had to do anything like this.

He finished and looked up. "This can't be true."

"Well," she said. "What if it is?"

"Then we've got ourselves a problem."

Lydia stared up at the ceiling. "Yes," she said to no one. "Yes, I think we do."

The magnitude began to tumble into view piece by piece, like broken stones skidding down a gully. One thing hit onto something else onto something else onto something else. And pretty soon, so many stones were broken free and falling that there wasn't a place to move over and get out of the way.

"They'll want every detail." L.R. scrubbed his fingers over a spot on his head that must have, some time in the past, been graced with thick hair. "No evidence is ever enough in cases like this."

Outside it was mild and fragrant for October, warm for evening, a tangle of blue jay complaint and wood thrush song. Finally Lydia voiced the awful thing she kept learning over and over again as she counseled, the awful possibility she had ignored after Shelby had given her Charlie's name. "A child almost never accuses without there being some truth behind it."

"Yes," he said. "I know that, too."

She stared out the window waiting for him to say something more, thinking of the powder-puff game and homecoming festivities and everything the students were celebrating this week.

"Charlie is such a good teacher. A good person. I've known him since he was splashing in puddles," L.R. said, his voice edged with despair. "Known him since he was learning to line up the ferrules on his fishing rod."

"A lot of people have told me that. It's one reason I—" She caught herself. *That's one reason I let my guard down with him in the first place.*

"You know what Charlie said when I interviewed him for his job?" L.R. said. "'I'm tired of the college politics. I just want to be someplace I can teach.' I was so impressed when he told me that."

Neither of them dared say aloud what they both were thinking. *Do you think he could have done it?*

L.R.'s face was deeply lined, gone gray with grief. "Never been so glad to see a man come home, start giving himself to the place he grew up in. Never been so sure when I hired him that what I was doing was the right thing."

Lydia braced herself against the table. She realized they were speaking of Charlie in the past tense, as if he were already gone.

"I've done what I had to, L.R. He needs you. Please don't you lose faith in him, too."

"When the social workers interview Shelby, they'll want a neutral location and a police officer here in plainclothes. Can you get Shelby here first thing tomorrow? I know they'll want to do it as soon as I give this report to them."

She swallowed. Hard. Made the commitment that she would bring the girl. "Yes."

"She'll tell the truth about it? She'll testify?"

"She's said she will."

"And you'll sit in with her?"

"I'll do anything you need me to do."

"Let's keep a lid on this thing as much as we can," L.R. said. "This isn't going to be any good for the school. If the *Democrat Reflex* gets hold of it, this place will be a madhouse. Not a word to Gritton, of course."

Lydia nodded. She didn't need to say anything else aloud. They were each of them thinking the same thing: *Everything this touches is going to fall apart.*

"Our first interest is in protecting Shelby from all this," L.R. said.

"Yes." Lydia rocked forward and back, forward and back. "Yes, of course it is."

L.R. had just picked up the telephone to make the call when a loud *pop* reverberated down the hall. It sounded as loud as a shot against the ominous long silence that followed it. Then came the sound of frail, hard music as broken glass fell somewhere.

And, for a moment, the two of them stared at each other, each wondering if someone had found out, if this was already happening because of Charlie.

"What was that?" L.R. asked Lydia.

"I don't know."

Out in the hallway, they glanced wildly about, searching for something amiss. But Riley McCaskill, the night janitor, had already locked every classroom door. An entire row of them up the A-hall—eighteen to be exact—and each one of them had been fastened tight.

In the dark hallway, Mo Eden stood transfixed, a red plastic biohazard box in her arms.

"Mo?" Lydia hurried toward her. "Are you okay?"

"I'm fine. Did you hear that?"

"We did."

"I had to sign off on those tetanus inoculation certifi-cates. Took me an hour longer than it was supposed to. I was just taking these empty vials to the car."

"Sounded like somebody shot out a front window to me." L.R. kept his back to the wall.

"I've had plenty of experience hearing gunshots. I grew up with my brother Baxter, the big-shot game bird hunter of St. Clair County. This was something else, Lon Ralph." Mo was one of only a privileged few who knew what the L. and R. stood for in the principal's name.

"Where'd it come from?" Lydia glanced from one end of the hallway to the other.

"The Home Ec room maybe?"

"That's what I think, too."

"Stay up against the wall," Nibarger said. Lydia let her-self and Mo be pressed into the lockers behind him. "Just in case."

As they crept along, the very familiarity of these hall-ways felt false. Up ahead an eerie orange light flickered, off again, on again, for a moment only half bright, a liquid moving color.

Lydia could smell something burning. Mo fished for her cell phone in her pocket. "I'll get the fire department." She began to punch in numbers.

When they reached the door in question, L.R. hopped on

one foot and yanked off his shoe. It registered only briefly that the principal was wearing yellow socks. How odd to see his big toe, its ragged toenail thrusting out through one of several unraveling holes.

"I'm breaking in." He pounded his Hush Puppie loafer against the window in the door. The heel bounced off, useless. He turned to them again. "And while I do, find me something that will hold water. We've got some big soup tureens in the Home Ec room, don't we?" He hauled off and banged the window with his fist. "*Ouch.*"

"Get back, Lon Ralph. Let me do it." Mo practically shoved him out of the way with her hip. "You can't fool around with this tempered glass." She raised the biohazard box she'd been carrying, flung it with both arms, as hard as she could, at the window. The glass imploded and fell in one wave, taking itself down. Smoke poured out of the opening.

"Here." Nibarger reached in to unlock the door.

"Not yet. Now this is when you use your shoe." Lydia took it from him. The glass left hanging looked like the edges of tiny ceramic tile, held in place by what remained of the wire mesh. With his loafer, she began to knock out pieces around the perimeter. Somewhere in the distance, a fire alarm began to blare.

L.R. grappled past her, reached the handle on the inside. He twisted the deadbolt and they were in. Around their feet, a dozen or so small fires still burned. A stack of graded nutrition tests had ignited. Flames licked one end of a bookshelf against the far wall. Seconds after the alarm began, the automatic sprinkler began to swirl water down on their heads.

Sirens, which had first been only a rising hum in the distance, now split the air with their wails. The St. Clair County pumper truck lumbered up outside. Behind it, the hook-and-ladder truck rolled in, followed by a dozen different cars owned by members of the volunteer ladder team.

In moments it seemed, gawkers from all over Shadrach had assembled. Lydia recognized people from as far away as Still Family Mountain and Boilerhead Road. Someone shined a searchlight in her eyes through the broken window, temporarily blinding her. Red-and-blue emergency lights throbbed, blazing against truck chrome and treetops as rescue and salvage vehicles parked at haphazard angles in the street.

"You know what this stench reminds me of?" L.R. flagged his arms through the smoke as if he were trying to find them. "Thirty years ago I went off and left the popcorn maker turned on all night at the Rialto. Came back the next day and this is what met me. Burnt corn. Smelled up the whole theater."

"Good grief, Lon Ralph," Mo said. "You could spare us the historical details right now, you know that?"

"Rialto seats smelled like scorched popcorn for over three decades. Up until Old Man Hardy decided he had to have cup holders and finally put new seats in."

The door swung open and in marched Captain Judd Ogle of the Shadrach Volunteer Fire Department, brandishing an ax.

Lydia, Maureen, and the principal stood there in street clothes, covered with ashes and wet, feeling victorious, but looking very small. Towering over them stood Captain Ogle in full fire-resistant Nomex, vast and formidable, the strips of safety-yellow reflective trim etching the fold of his forearms, his yellow helmet rammed low and businesslike over his eyes.

"I'm Fireground Commander for this mission," he announced. "Anything I need to know as my teams get into place?"

"Just *this*," L.R. gestured toward the debris they kept stumbling over on the floor. "The fire is out."

Lydia crossed the room and flipped the light switch. The fluorescents came on, fierce and bright. Charred sweet-corn ears littered the floor. Ogle picked one up; it was smoking from one end like a gigantic cigar.

"Well, I'll be jumped up." Ogle pulled his chin, squeezed it together at the bottom. "Thought we were dealing with Molotov cocktails here. Guess not. These came right out of somebody's cornfield, didn't they?"

One of Ogle's sergeants had tagged along as rear guard. Two uniformed police officers flanked the door. The sergeant said, "Looks like yellow bantam corn. Some good crop. Maybe Joe Wester's place down along Barn Hollow."

"Well, now. I don't figure Wester's got anything to do with this. That corn looks like out-of-county stuff to me." Ogle shook his head. "It's a shame. All dressed up in my shake-and-bakes for a lot less than a bushel of ears." He held one up. "See this?" The silk and husks had been twisted into a wick on the top end. "Missouri folks used to light these and use them for flashlights back in the old days. I can see igniting one or two of these things as a prank. Would have been easy enough to do with a cigarette lighter." Ogle's mouth went thin. "But this many?"

L.R. picked one up, sniffed it, recoiled. "They've been soaking in something. Paint thinner, maybe? Kerosene?" He handed it over. "What do you think?"

Ogle sniffed, too, and nodded. "Kerosene would be my guess. Somebody's doctored up a whole bunch of corncobs, all right."

It seemed so incongruous, a uniformed man kicking aside rolled, charred corncobs with heavy boots and Nomex-clad legs as big around as buckets. He certainly wouldn't need his ax for *this*.

"Hey, Captain," somebody bellowed from outside. "You'd better have a look at what we've got out here."

Toilet paper scalloped through the lacy branches and billowed like confetti from at least five different trees. As they stood in the yard surveying the purple spray-painted letters on the mortar-and-brick school walls, Lydia saw Brad Gritton's car screech to a halt behind the pumper truck. He threw open the door, climbed out, and strode toward Lydia with purposeful steps.

L.R. intercepted him. "What are you doing here, Gritton?"

"You know what I'm doing," he said, looking past L.R.'s shoulder at Lydia. "I'm doing what I teach all my journalism students to do. I'm listening to my police scanner and chasing fire trucks. I get most of my best stories that way."

"Well, you don't have to pursue this story any further," L.R. said and even Lydia bristled at how defensive he sounded. "I was here for a late meeting with Miss Porter when the ruckus started. We've got everything under control. There certainly doesn't need to be any reporting about *this*."

But just as Nibarger said the words, Mo Eden, who had been yanking strands of toilet paper out of tree limbs, cried out. "Oh my *heavens*." She staggered toward a body swinging heavily from a rope.

Captain Ogle looped his big arm around her shoulders. "It's okay, Miz Eden. It isn't anything *alive*."

"Not hanging like that, it isn't alive." She backed away. "Of course it isn't."

"Look at it real careful. Again."

She did, squinting. And then, she must have recognized it because she yelped, "Oh, get her *down*. Please take her *down*."

So began the careful, tedious task of bringing Mo's CPR dummy out of the tree. The dummy was dressed in an article of clothing no one had seen before—a 1950s house-coat with huge cabbage roses, snap buttons, and chartreuse grosgrain trim. A sash girded its length from left shoulder to right hip joint.

"Of all the nights not to lock my office." Mo held out her arms for it.

A sign nailed to the sycamore trunk read SHADRACH'S HOMECOMING QUEEN 2003. SHADRACH STUDENTS LOVE THEIR ATHLETIC SUPPORTERS. And that, *ahem*, questionable item, an unclaimed athletic supporter, was wrapped around the dummy's head like a crown.

Ogle plucked off his helmet in disappointment and tossed it to the ground.

Shadrach Up In Flames, the graffiti on the bricks proclaimed. It would take at least a month to get it off again. Abednego Blazers, Victory All The Way!!!!!

"Got my whole department out here. Should've known it'd be nothing but a homecoming rivalry stunt."

Sensing a need for a bit of face saving, L.R. clasped Ogle's palm with true gratitude, vigorously pumping hands with him. "You are our public servants," he said. "This could have been a life-threatening situation. It's a credit to you that you ran in to take charge. Our first responders."

With a sigh, Lydia turned to leave. It had been an agonizingly long day and all she wanted at this point was to go home.

"Lydia. Wait a minute."

She turned toward the voice and discovered that L.R.'s

words hadn't deterred Brad at all. Now that the officers were clearing out, here he came after her with his narrow pad flipped open and a pen drawn to take notes. She shot him a pleasant, patient smile. She had no reason to think that he might ask her about anything other than the events on the school lawn. "What is it you need?"

Lydia felt mean but she couldn't help but find him amusing, a predictable guy who had been around the school forever, part of the furniture. He had no poetry in his soul.

"Call me crazy," he said, giving her an apologetic grin. "Call it a sixth sense. A journalist's training. But I'm not ready to give up on this yet."

"What?"

"I'd like you to tell me what's really going on here tonight."

"The Abednego kids teepeed the school, kidnapped the CPR dummy, and threw burning corn into a broken window. That's what happened."

"No, Lydia," he said. "I think there's more."

She did a double-take, stared at him.

"What on earth would give you that idea?"

"I saw the police report. On a night when the students were playing in a powder-puff football game, you and Nibarger were here together, having a late meeting at the school. I think it might be significant to know why."

The blood froze in Lydia's veins. "My meetings are confidential," she told him. "I owe that to my students. You know that."

"You don't deny it, though, do you? You don't deny that there is something going on behind closed doors at this school?"

Behind closed doors. All of this was just beginning. Already it felt like it would never end, like it would never stop.

Brad, poor Brad, who had no idea what he had stumbled upon. And suddenly he didn't seem quite so harmless anymore.

"I care about you, Lydia. If there's something going on that affects you, I think I ought to know about it."

She felt like everything was pressing in on her from every side. She shook her head.

"Please, Lydia. Talk to me."

She had started forward with what she had thought she was supposed to do. And now she felt like one of the Israelites being told to walk into the Promised Land, finding out she was stepping into a valley of giants instead. These past two days, there had been one giant after another after another.

"No," she said with honest grief. "I can't."

CHAPTER EIGHT

———— ❧ ————

*F*riday morning, the day after the powder-puff game, the senior girls were still chattering about their play-calling in the huddles, their defensive strategies, and one forty-four-yard field goal. A number of them hobbled proudly around the school, displaying their injuries, ranging from crushed toenails and bruised elbows to Charlotte Marcus, who had been rushed to the Orthopedic Clinic in Osceola with a bruised groin.

When the bell sounded promptly at 10:30 for the pep rally, a heightened sense of determination filled the halls. Not one student had missed the boarded windows in the Home Ec room. Not one had missed the thready burn marks on the floor or the yellow tape that read DO NOT CROSS—POLICE LINE or the scrawled mess of graffiti that could be read all the way from Riley McCaskill's apartment near the Show Me Kwik Gas on the corner of Montgomery. In great milling throngs, the students stopped by their lockers, found friends, and made their way purposefully toward the gym.

Tonight at the homecoming football game, they planned to defeat the Abednego Blazers. They planned to disprove those audacious spray-painted remarks on the walls outside. They planned to uphold the honor of their school.

Kids tromped up the wooden bleachers by the dozens, sounding more like a herd of Missouri feeder cattle than human teenagers. The band director, Dr. Duncan Minor from a music school in Kansas City, lifted his baton, counted off the beats and, with *a one a two a one two three four,* the mighty Shadrach Fire-Rattler Marching Band blared into a trumpet-heavy version of "Na, Na, Hey, Hey, Kiss Him Good-Bye."

No matter how foul Sam Leavitt's mood, the activity and noise at the pep assembly made for good video shots. Sam was taping as an assignment for Mr. Gritton's journalism class. He took quick, punchy angles, funny details that could be edited into the finished footage in the Student News lab. A close-up floor-level shot of the cheerleaders' shoes moving in routine, bouncing, pointing, disappearing for a high-kick into the glare of the lights. The shining baldness and bushy gray hair of Dr. Minor, who looked as if he were wearing a silvery Christmas wreath around the crown of his head. The skate-boarder kids with chains from belt loops to pockets, their bored eyes as they slouched against the banner that proclaimed GO FIRE-RATTLERS!

Everywhere Sam looked his friends were clapping and yelling and swaying, a sea of expectant bodies clad in red and blue.

All the other girls had shown up last night to applaud Sam's powder-puff cheerleading. All the juniors and seniors playing on the team were there, and the other ones, too—their faces smeared in tribal red-and-blue paint, their senior year, '04 or '05 or '06, scribbled wildly on their cheeks.

You'd think Shelby would have shown up, too.

Whitney Allen had driven him crazy with her fancy cornrows of little braids that striped straight back on her head like the markings on a sparrow, bouncing around him while he scanned the bleachers and searched for the one person he most wanted to see.

"How come she isn't here, Sam? Are you guys having a fight?"

"No, we're not."

"Yeah, everybody I know says you are. Are you breaking up?"

"Do I look like I'm breaking up?"

"Maybe."

"Where is she?"

"I don't know."

To top that off, the male cheerleading squad, which he hadn't really wanted to join in the first place, had decided they had to try a pyramid. When they told him they wanted him on top, he had uttered a few choice words that would have made his mother wash his mouth out with harsh antibacterial cleanser.

Since he'd reacted violently to that idea, they put him on the bottom instead. And exactly what he'd known would happen, happened.

They fell.

All seven, on top of him. All seven of whom were on the *real* football team and who had been working to lift weights and bulk up since the week of two-a-days they'd had last spring.

He'd torn his mother's skirt and his ribcage ached like somebody had sucker punched him. He could only breathe in about halfway.

The Shadrach cheerleaders were doing just as fine a job riling up the student body as Whit A. had done riling *him*. "Se-niors! Se-niors! *How do you feel?!*"

An entire section of rowdies pounded on the bleachers and screamed back, "We feel good, oh yeah we-feel-so-*good UUhhh*."

Any minute now and Mr. Nibarger would speak out over the public-address system to announce the names of this year's homecoming court. Sam had wangled the special assignment of video taping today's rally from Mr. Gritton well over two weeks ago. He wanted to escape the ranks of the football team long enough to stand out on the gym floor where he could give Shelby a hard time.

There could be two hundred other kids sailing paper airplanes or saving seats and screaming or bumping each other off the bleachers, but whenever Shelby walked in, something happened to him. *Zing.* Something hitched in his lungs and made it hurt to breathe, even if he *hadn't* been fallen on by seven hefty team members. Whenever she walked in, he couldn't help smiling a little more, laughing a little louder. And the whole time he was talking to anybody else, he didn't have to look to see where Shelby was standing. He just *knew.*

Because feeling that way about a girl could get scary when you were seventeen years old, Sam Leavitt was always coming up with new ways to tease her. There had been the rubber-band fight he'd let her win after they'd tied about a hundred of Mrs. Jones's rubber-band stash into a chain. There had been the week he'd memorized her locker combination and had stacked it full of pansy flats from the Wal-Mart garden section. There had been the night the whole football team had driven by her house and had left three dozen warm Krispy Kreme glazed donuts stuck to the front bay window.

He had a lot of fun, bugging her like that.

Sam had a big plan to record *her* today while he was supposed to be taping other things instead. He knew her cheeks would get rosy and she'd turn all flustered when he trailed her with the camcorder, getting all the angles of her face that he loved, watching her through one squinted eye.

Only, where was she?

The huge gym was packed with all his friends and classmates, but without Shelby the place might as well have been empty. And Sam cared about getting footage of the pep assembly without her about as much as he cared about having his wisdom teeth extracted.

"Hey, Leavitt," Coach Fortney hollered across the gym. "You tape what you need and then you go get your tie on. I want you over here with the rest of the football team. Gritton knows better than to take my kids away at a time like this."

This is an *assignment,* he'd been planning to say. But he only shrugged his shoulders, nodded *yeah, I'm coming,* pivoted the lens away.

"Welcome students and alumni of Shadrach High School." Patrice Saunders rose from the faculty seating, took the microphone in hand, which surprised everyone. "We are thrilled to have you join us for our 2003 Homecoming Celebration."

"Where's Nibarger?" Because Sam would be filming, they'd given him a schedule. "She's not the one who's supposed to be up there talking."

Johnny Nagle, one of the skate-boarders leaning defensively against the state-championship sign, lifted his saggy-jeans-clad hip off the wall and readjusted. "Hey, man, I heard he's in a meeting. Some big emergency."

Mrs. Saunders proceeded in a sing-song voice they would all remember for years to come. "A good number of Shadrach alumni have journeyed home this week to help us celebrate. They are here in our little town taking a trip down memory lane." She droned on with an overview of this year's football season, lauding the team for their wins and ignoring the losses. At last, she relinquished her microphone to Coach Fortney, who took the podium. He introduced his players one by one as some kids cheered and other kids hooted with derision. "Will Devine, tailback, has pluck and grit to get the job done."

"Yeah," somebody whispered, "he'll tail you back, all right."

"Daniel Maher, defensive end, scored the game-clinching touchdown on an interception against Downs High last week. Adam Buttars, kicker, has scored five extra points and field goals of 34 and 43 yards so far this season. Sam Leavitt, tight end, is a solid blocker and a terrific receiver, including the 54-yard reception in the Van Alstine game . . ."

One by one they mounted the platform, received a certificate from Fortney that had been signed by the superintendent of schools, while Sam mentally promised he'd take out anybody who made comments about *tight end*. He stepped up with his minicam rolling, his ribs still aching and his tie still AWOL. He got a great shot of Coach Fortney's nose hairs as he handed over the certificate of merit for Sam's senior football season. The pin for his letter jacket would come in December at the banquet.

Once Fortney had finished, Mrs. Saunders introduced Amy Sondergroth, the president of the student council, and the students settled down. Amy adjusted the microphone, stepped away wincing when it started to buzz. When somebody somewhere adjusted the sound, she pressed her mouth close and relied on her notes. With a hollow, ringing voice she announced, "Students of Shadrach High, I'd like to introduce you to *your* choices for the 2003 homecoming court!" The place went wild. "When I call your name, please step forward."

And so she began.

The stands erupted into cheers and screaming each time a name was called. At least fifteen different kids had to hug, raise a fist in victory, or clap-on-the-back and jump around as the candidate started down. Everything was going fine until Amy announced, "And *your* choice for sophomore princess, Shelby Tatum!"

There was the initial outburst of applause and then . . . nothing.

Sam, who had been holding the pain in his side and panning the student body with the camcorder in hopes of catching somebody, stopped filming in shock. *Where was she?*

"Shelby's absent," somebody bellowed. A few people were still clapping and looking around. The applause dwindled, like splatters of intermittent rain.

"Shelby's trying to avoid Leavitt," Devine hooted, his voice cutting through everything else. "Ask *him* why she isn't here."

Amy rattled the papers as she flipped to a new page. "Okay, that's fine. We'll just go on to another—"

The double doors to the hall slammed open. Sam began

to shoot again; he wasn't even sure why. The apparatus hung heavy in his hand, and he used it. He began to pan the doorway as the lens brought everything into focus.

He'd pointed his minicam and found himself photographing another camera. This one a nice Pentax, taking stills, clicking away. A couple of people he didn't recognize wore laminated badges. Press passes from the *Shadrach Democrat Reflex*. His first thought: *Why would they care this much about the homecoming court?*

But he saw quickly that this wasn't about the assembly at all. The man with the Pentax approached Amy. Someone had a broadcast microphone, too, with well-marked call letters from the AM hottest-hits station in Osceola.

"Someone called us this morning with an anonymous tip," said the woman with the microphone to their student-body president. The man with the Pentax clicked away.

"What?" Amy was lost.

"We have from a reliable source that a Shadrach student is accusing a teacher of molesting her. Do you have any comment about that?"

Amy tried to shield herself with her hands. "I don't know any—"

Patrice Saunders wrapped an arm around the girl and safeguarded her, steering her down off the platform. "Who gave you permission to come in here and do this? You know we have security rules. All visitors sign in at the office."

One man flashed his pass at her. "You know me, Patrice.

Dan Parker from the *Democrat Reflex*. I always cover the school news."

"Not today, you don't cover it. Now go on back where you came from."

"You might as well give us the story. If this is true, it's gonna be big. Something that might bring all the networks down on Shadrach."

Sam was still taping when Brad Gritton climbed down off the bleachers. He focused the lens on his journalism teacher, who came striding purposefully toward him. "Cut the camera, Sam," Gritton said while the camera lens focused automatically on his nose. "There's no reason you need to be taping this."

Sam punched the Pause button. The screen went black. Sam watched his teacher move with determination toward the knot of people and microphones.

"You know how it's supposed to work," Sam heard him say. "If this is true, then you'll have to publish it from courthouse reports. Not from some hearsay evidence."

"We're just the little guys. I think we have the right to know first."

"Hey." Johnny Nagle came up from the wall, out of his bored slouch. He fished for a wallet in his baggy back pocket and flipped it open. "I've got pictures." He pulled out a whole stack of 2x3-inch school photos that he'd collected from his friends. "This is my entire collection. All the hot babes in the school. One of these girls just might be the one you're looking for."

"Let me see those." Parker swiped at them but he grabbed empty air. Nagle, always one to make an extra buck, had yanked them aside.

"I didn't say you could have them. They're up for sale. Fifteen bucks a shot. You want them, you've got to pay."

Brad Gritton was at the podium almost before anyone had seen him coming.

"Can you confirm this rumor about the school, Gritton?" And Parker was close enough to Patrice Saunders and the microphone that the question broadcast to the rafters. "Or can you deny it?"

But Sam saw that the journalism teacher wasn't listening. He was following the electrical cord from where it left the metal base and snaked across the floor beneath a long, narrow strip of duct tape. Dr. Minor, the band director, who was much too far away to come to the bodily rescue of the staff on the floor, lifted his hands, the left one gripping the baton.

"Can you deny that school officials are meeting with police and the Department of Health and Human Services right now, trying to decide what to do?"

"Number *three,*" the band director mouthed soundlessly so his high school band members would be able to find the music. "*LOUD.*"

"Can you confirm that there are going to be charges filed, Gritton? Can you tell us if this is a credible accusation?"

Zip. Up came the length of tape. Brad Gritton jerked the plug out of the wall.

The sound system went dead. Three hundred kids were no longer privy to their conversation.

"Now I'm going to tell you what I think about you coming in like this, Parker," Gritton said, and nobody heard him except for Sam Leavitt and Johnny Nagle and about a dozen others who happened to be standing in his path as he strode angrily back. "It all started during CNN and Desert Storm. Journalism as an unfolding drama instead of a fact-finding mission. Everybody's in a rush to be the first to say something, even if they aren't sure what they're saying yet."

Parker came right back at him. "If you had an ounce of professional loyalty, Gritton, you would be the one turning in this story."

"You think you're going to discover anything by coming in here and shouting about what you know?"

Up in the stands, Dr. Minor marked the downbeat of the song with a heavy stroke of his arms and a slash of his baton. The Mighty Fire-Rattler Marching Band broke into a staggering rendition of "We Will Rock You," rivaling in both finesse and volume any version that might have ever been played for the Kansas City Chiefs at Arrowhead Stadium or for Kurt Warner and the St. Louis Rams at the Trans World Dome.

The entire Shadrach student body rose to its feet, sensing only that everyone needed to stand up for the honor of the school. *Stomp-stomp CLAP. Stomp-stomp CLAP.* And then, at the top of their lungs, they began to sing, even if they didn't know the words. *Da da-da-da young boy da dada-da tempo . . .*

Sam started the minicam again. The musical interlude, as deafening as it was, and Brad Gritton's interruption, had given Patrice Saunders the moment she needed to compose herself. Sam taped again as, "If there is any news to be released about this school, we will notify the press in an official statement this afternoon," she informed the invading microphone with a voice that could freeze Springfield in August.

Later, when others would look at Sam's video, they would see that it was Brad Gritton, the journalism teacher, and Charlie Stains, the woodshop teacher, who began to move up and down the bleachers, touching students with great care on the shoulders, releasing them in rows so that no one would get hurt. In Sam's video, they would see the two male teachers standing guard together with crossed arms as the students of Shadrach High trampled their way down the steps in hoards, headed to their next classes.

But because Sam hadn't filmed this, no one would ever know that, after the gym had cleared, Charlie Stains stood alone in one corner, his spine pressed against the wall, his face gone as gray as the cement blocks behind him. He stood with his eyes closed against the world, as if he might soak up just one more piece of this place before he had to walk out.

And, of course, the whispering in the hallways began as soon as the Shadrach students cleared the gym.

CHAPTER NINE

They passed each other as Lydia came winding her way through students in B-hall and Charlie was heading toward the door.

As if she felt his gaze on her, she lifted her eyes to his.

He stopped so fast when she looked at him that, like dominoes, people ran into him from behind.

For one beat, another, they stared. Then her eyes jerked away.

"Lydia."

In his arms, Charlie carried a box filled with personal belongings he had packed out of his classroom. On the top of the pile was the Billy Bob Big Mouth Bass, a plastic fish that, when you punched a button, turned toward you to sing its song. "Don't Worry, Be Happy."

Fifteen months he'd spent settling in at Shadrach High School and this was what he had to show for it. One Dell computer carton filled with his junk. The boat he'd managed to win in a church auction. One woman he had thought trusted him enough to spend her life with him. And this knotted-up, physical sensation in his belly, like one of those deep, painful dreams where you're in a public place and don't have any clothes on.

Even if he didn't have anything to hide from, he still wanted to, and couldn't. He felt helpless. Exposed. Vaguely scraped and guilty on the inside, as if parts of everything he had ever done were wrong.

There were so many things to say. So many regrets to share. "You're leaving," she said.

He nodded as the kids began to move around both of them like creek water rushing around rocks. "I am."

She said the words as if she needed to take great gulps of air around them, like the fish they'd caught by hand and hauled out onto shore. "They've let you go."

"L.R. requested it. A leave of absence. But we all know he'll release me from my contract as soon as he can."

By the brusque way L.R. had stepped into his classroom and launched immediately into speech, Charlie knew he must have been practicing it all the way up the hall.

You understand, don't you? You understand what I have to ask you to do?

He hadn't answered. He'd just kept packing the box. In went a battery-operated pencil sharpener, a small case of whittling tools, a half-full bottle of Gorilla Glue.

Charlie, you've done a fantastic job with these kids. It will only go into the record as a leave of absence, you know, until the investigation is over. Until everyone's figured out what's going on.

In the hall with Lydia, Charlie shoved the plastic fish down as far as it would go and began to fold shut the lid to the box, two sides down. He didn't want her looking at his belongings. You would have thought, by the way she focused on them, that they were the most fascinating things she'd ever seen.

"This is what L.R. wants," Charlie said to Lydia as she stood in front of him. Just a good-bye, a disappearance into the sunset. Clean and neat. Quiet and simple. The school district would be legally covered. "He asked what I would be doing with all my free time. I told him I had a new boat. I told him I would spend a lot of time out on the Brownbranch. Fishing. I don't know."

I put a call in to personnel this morning at the University of Missouri, L.R. had said. *I'm waiting for someone to phone me back. You know, I didn't check your references the first time. I had known you so long that I didn't think it necessary.*

I appreciate that, he'd answered with pain in his voice. *That means a lot to me.*

Why is it you decided to leave your college professorship? You told me it was politics. We talked around it during your interview, but you never ever really said. Why did you really come back? Were you running from something?

I'm not much in the mood to rehash my work history right now, L.R.

Do I have something to worry about in my school? Did you touch that girl, Charlie?

As the students moved around Charlie and Lydia in the corridor, the stream of people pressed them closer toward each other. And he suddenly felt like he was gasping for air, with her being so near, as he hunched over the cardboard box like he had an abdominal wound. The lid wouldn't stay shut. He shoved it down, clamped his teeth together so hard that he figured she could see veins straining in his jaw.

Two people who had thought they had known each other so well. Two people who could list each other's allergies and ring size and favorite movies. Two people who had discussed fishing holes together and house plans and wedding dates. They stood in poignant wordlessness, as if they had never really ever talked to each other at all, as if someone else had been carrying the conversation, and now they were lost.

"Well," he said.

"Well," she said, clearing her throat. He could see her hands shaking.

And so they both understood it. Now, being alone together, there wasn't anything left to say.

"I'm sorry."

"Don't," she said. "Don't you apologize. When you apologize, it makes you sound like you're *wrong*."

He stepped past her.

"I'll come with you out to the car."

"That isn't necessary."

"I can't leave it this way, Charlie."

"Maybe you ought to."

"No."

"Someone will see you with me."

"Do you think that really matters to me right now?"

He didn't say *Suit yourself.* He just plodded past her, out toward the parking lot and let her make her own decision. He sensed her behind him and knew she was still there.

He didn't have the boat attached to his truck anymore. He had unhitched it and chocked the tires with rocks in his yard, where he had decided it would be safe. He jammed the computer box inside the truck bed and shoved a tool chest up against it so it wouldn't stand any chance of blowing out. "What I want to know is this," he suddenly said to her with censure. "Only one question I have to ask you."

"What?" She uncrossed her arms.

"I want to know if you believe that girl or if you believe me. I want to know which one of us you think is telling the truth."

She stood looking at him as if that question had come too fast, as if he had nailed her to the wall.

"Lydia?"

She started toward him again, taking up the last few steps between herself and the truck.

"Stay where you are," he said. "Don't move any closer until you answer."

She fumbled around for a moment. "Why would you even have to ask what I think?"

"You know why."

"Don't do this. Charlie, please."

He yanked open the driver's side and climbed in.

"You've agreed to commit your life to me. I need to know where this leaves us."

He held the door open until she answered. He gave her no time to fabricate a story or to temper her thoughts with careful words. Lydia had nothing else in mind that she could say; the words came blurting out. "No. I don't think that *girl's* telling me the truth, and I don't necessarily think *you* are, either."

"That's what I thought." After he slammed the door, Charlie cranked down the window like he was reeling in a fighter fish, as hard as he could. He popped the gas pedal, so frustrated he didn't stop to think that it would flood the engine when he tried to start it. "That's exactly what I thought."

"Don't you go yet," she said, taking the steps two at a time. "Look, you can't expect me to not question this. I'm just *human*."

"That's the problem with the whole world, isn't it? Everybody's just human."

"Charlie—"

"Don't you know I could have dealt with this, Lydia, if I knew that you were behind me?"

Lydia grabbed the door and opened it. "How could you say that? How could you make me be the responsible one?"

Like mist that settled heavy in the bottomlands and rose when sun warmed the air, all the things they could have said to each other and all the things that, to both of them, were unspeakable—*I can't stop thinking of the things Shelby said . . .*

I thought I could count on you to trust me.

Some doubts are too big to overcome, Charlie.

I needed you, Lydia, and you aren't there for me—disclosures, denials, admissions, guilt, shame mounted between them. There wasn't anything that could save what they had been.

Charlie stumbled up out of the truck and seized her, hauling her against him, locking his mouth against hers so hard that she tasted blood. Hip to hip, thigh to thigh, leg to leg, their shoulders straining.

"Stop it," she cried against his lips. "Just stop it. This doesn't make anything different."

"Lydia, you're shaking. Are you that afraid of me?"

"I want you to leave."

"From that kiss, it was hard for me to know it." His mouth twisted, but it wasn't a smile.

She slapped him, hard. He lurched back. Overhead the breeze came up and rattled the limbs like rake tines. "I won't be manhandled by you," she said.

The set of his jaw tightened. "That so?"

It took a tough man to stand before her without reacting, letting her see him broken and strong. But Charlie could be as tough as a log chain. As strong as a thick, broad white oak.

When he stumbled back into the truck and slammed the door, he couldn't stop his chest from heaving. On the sidewalk, the damp leaves smelled like steeping, pungent tea.

And Lydia just stood there, her eyes closed, as he ached to say her name. *Lyddie.*

He keyed the engine instead. The radio awakened with static. He stared at it a minute, expecting a Shadrach football rundown. When the radio didn't give it to him immediately, he took his frustration out on the knob, twisting it. AM stations crackled up from everywhere.

"John Ashcroft . . . if we pray . . . down three to two . . . new dessert menu . . . Joe knows . . . made the Anaheim Angels so . . . music up . . . in store for you . . . the problem with illegal game-bird baiting . . . believe Christ . . . it's Taco-riffic! . . . the Carnahan platform . . . final close-out sale, cash and carry . . ."

The sound stopped in one long hum as if the dial had honed in by itself.

"In other statewide news today, Missouri officials are continuing an investigation this hour after a St. Clair County student made claims that a high school teacher allegedly abused her—"

Charlie punched it off.

That radio report was the last sound between them. When he drove away, he left only the leaves at the curb behind him, whispering that he had been there.

CHAPTER TEN

───── ❧ ─────

*S*am Leavitt played into the third quarter of the home-coming game before the team trainer diagnosed his broken rib.

When Coach had lined them up in a two-point stance for warm-ups and assigned them to catch balls while they ran at half speed, Sam had forgotten everything except the battle-call to defeat the Abednego Blazers. His muscles were itching to burn.

The decibel level at the earlier assembly couldn't compare to the uproar from Shadrach fans now, their arch rivals in plain view and listening across the field. Rolls of crepe paper soared through the air and unfurled before the opposite team like gauntlets. For all the encouragement and hollering and passion, the two sides might as well have been tribal villages in a life-or-death standoff instead of students at a game.

By the time the Fire-Rattlers met helmet to helmet in the

huddle, there wasn't time for Sam to think about the bizarre journalist invasion or the angry pain in his side. The corncob burning had incited a riot atmosphere among his classmates and his team. Sam wanted to perform.

Every time he thought about Whitney and the questions she'd asked him—*Where's Shelby?*—he wanted to hit something. And so that's just what he did.

In the first quarter he made three bone-crushing blocks, one that laid a kid out and opened a hole for Will Devine to make a thirty-two-yard run up the left sideline for a touchdown.

During the second quarter, with the sky fading to black and high banks of stadium lights streaming onto the field, Coach Fortney called his number for an inside release. On Josh Dailey's snap-count, Sam took one short jab step off the line of scrimmage, escaped from the Abednego defensive end with a brutal forearm blow to an inside shoulder, and sprinted upfield.

Josh rocketed him a ball that hit square between the 8 and the 4 on his jersey. Sam wrapped his arms around it and took off. Two plays later Adam kicked his first field goal of the game.

At halftime in the locker room, which sounded like a barnyard and didn't smell much better, they were already high-fiving and exchanging victory grunts.

"Way to let 'em have it, Dailey."

"Did you see that hit Leavitt laid on the cornerback?"

"Those guys are going home with their *tails* between their *legs*."

"What is this?" Coach bellowed at them. "You think you're finished for the day? You think it all ends here?"

"Well—"

"You've got the entire population of Shadrach out there in the stands depending on you and you think it's time you can stop and celebrate along with them?"

They plopped their helmets on the benches, heads bent, and let him rage at them. He showed them diagrams, gave each one of them individual criticism. By the time he was finished they felt like they'd fallen ten points behind instead of the other way around. In one connected, surging unit, they blasted up out of the locker room and smashed through the red paper banner.

Four minutes into the third quarter, Coach called Will Devine's number again and Sam stutter-stepped into a perfect fake, drawing off a 225-pound Abednego linebacker. The linebacker rushed at him while Josh shoveled the ball toward his teammate.

At the last possible second, an Abednego player caught on and wheeled in Will's direction. Sam blasted forward, throwing his right forearm into a brutal left-shoulder block.

The play unfolded just the way they'd practiced it. The Abednego defensive line piled in on top of Sam while Will broke free. Somewhere in the distance, Sam heard the crowd going wild. Above him, above everything else, above the massive dinosaur of pads and sweat and bodies that pinned him into the ground, above the crepe paper flying and the blinding glare of the lights, hovered the pain.

Sam couldn't breathe and he couldn't stand up. He tried, and went down on all fours. "Hey, Leavitt," he heard someone calling through the blood pounding in his ears. "You okay?"

He rolled over onto his back. The stinking bodies were gone and he could see banks of lights blaring down on him from every direction. They whirled above him, moving, drawing circles. He had no sense of time passing until Deanna Woodruff, the team's trainer, floated over him with her six-pack of Gatorade bottles and a sports towel. Somewhere far away the band played. And the next thing he knew, someone was shoving his ribcage, bulldozer pressure. He came up out of himself. He snarled at everybody standing within ten miles. "That's *it*. You *found it, okay?*"

Faces swam in and out in front of him. He squeezed his eyes shut. And heard, "Thing's already been swollen. It isn't a new injury. Leavitt, has this been bothering you before?"

Sam winced and opened his eyes again. "Just since"—he grimaced—"yesterday's powder-puff."

They lifted him, their shoulders thrust beneath his armpits, human crutches bearing him along. A smattering of polite applause erupted from the stands.

Deanna rummaged through the first-aid box on the Fire-Rattler sidelines, helped him off with his jersey, and began to girdle his middle with tape. She had him halfway bound up like a mummy when, suddenly, he lifted his eyes to the stands and there she was.

"Shelby!" he hollered, jerking away from Deanna, not making it very far. He left what felt like most of his epidermis on a scant ten inches of athletic tape.

Sam couldn't be sure whether it was the pain or the Vioxx he'd just downed or the way he could see Shelby clutching the railing that made him woozy. Deanna batted his elbow out of the way. "Get your arm down, Leavitt. Stop moving."

"Shelby. Down here!"

"Fortney wants me to get you back out there. I've got about two more minutes to tape this rib."

Shelby either wouldn't or couldn't hear him. Five or six rows of people turned in answer to his voice, but Shelby wasn't one of them. She stood exactly where she had appeared, between Joe Rex Hannibal, who made his living cutting meat at Winn-Dixie, and Sharla Crabtree, head bookkeeper at the Shadrach Bank and Trust, looking out across the Shadrach football field as if she gazed out over an endless nothing. He tried to unwind himself like a spool of thread. "Dee, let me go a minute. She's right there."

"Tough luck." Deanna grabbed one end of the tape and rewound him, forcing him to the bench. "Get your head in the game."

By the time he was able to stand up again and pivot toward the bleachers, she was disappearing. She backed away, stepping down into the aisle behind Joe Rex and Sharla, a solid row of standing loyal fans. She didn't appear again.

"Leavitt." Coach gripped his shoulder and held it a minute with concern. "You gonna be up to this?"

"Sure I am," Sam said without turning. Then said it loud enough again to convince himself. "Sure I am."

"Okay, then." Fortney whacked him on the butt. "Get on out there. You're in."

And the only thing Sam could think about as he ran to join the huddle was Shelby's face; the number he thought he'd seen painted on her cheek. Not her senior season like the rest of the girls, no. A football number, a tight-end number. 84. The jersey number he'd been wearing all year.

∞

INSIDE THE HIGH SCHOOL during the football game, Riley McCaskill had his floor polisher cranked up full speed. It wove back and forth across the gym floor, vibrating in loud circles, as Riley polished the boards for the dance.

Earlier this evening, there had been plenty of people around. Volunteer parents had been busy arranging tables, flopping open tablecloths and carrying finger foods to the Home Ec refrigerator. Student-council members had spent hours balancing on ladders, hanging disco balls, and draping black paper from the light fixtures. But now, except for Riley and the disc jockey who had been testing his sound system, most people had finished their jobs and had filtered away.

Because so many had been coming and going, the downstairs side door just outside the gym had been left unlocked. Above the constant whine of the floor polisher, no one could have heard as this door clicked open and someone slipped inside.

Every light in downstairs C-hall had been left blazing. A figure moved into the stairwell and began to climb the steps into darkness.

After enough time had passed for eyes to adjust at the top, the form slowly, silently began to make its way along the upstairs C-hall.

A wavering, pale beam switched on. Apparently unsatisfied with the amount of light being given out, the intruder smacked the old flashlight in a palm. But the beam stayed just as pale, just as weak.

The flashlight began to play over the locker numbers. 145. 146. 147. And, as if the figure had finally figured out which direction it needed to go, it began to move a little faster.

The person didn't touch any locker handles. He didn't rattle any metal doors. But when he came to Shelby Tatum's locker, he stopped, focused the flashlight beam on the combination lock, and double-checked a square of paper in his pocket. He redirected the light on the locker number, as if to make sure. When he was certain he'd found the right one, he began to twirl the dial, fiddling with the sequence of numbers, not certain that he knew how to make the tumblers fall into place.

Nobody stopped him, nobody questioned him, as he fumbled with the combination at least five times before finally wrenching open the door. When he did, a great tumble of Shelby's things fell out at him—textbooks with doodles on their covers, a jumble of folded notes, assorted papers, Sam Leavitt's senior picture, and a Claire's lip gloss. Three different sweaters dangled from hooks below.

The man knew he'd found the right locker because he recognized the smell of her pink lotion. Something she bought at Bath and Body Works. He didn't know the name of it, but he would recognize the stuff anywhere.

No sense leaving things intact here. No sense taking any chances. He had come prepared. He began to rake things off the shelves into a plastic trash bag.

When he had shoved everything in, he tied the handles in a knot. He chuckled under his breath. This wasn't even heavy. He had been worrying about that.

He used the light to find his way to the stairwell again. He would have to watch out for the janitor and the dance preparations down there. It had been a long time since he had been to a dance. He punched the flashlight button and the shaft of light was gone. He stood, gripping the banister with one hand and hanging on to the bag of Shelby's things in the other. He waited for his eyes to adjust again.

Without making a sound, he descended into the light. He stopped, listening for the floor polisher to make sure he wouldn't be seen. Somewhere off to his right, he could still hear it.

He slipped out of the school the same way he had come.

CHAPTER ELEVEN

Lydia hadn't meant for anyone to know she was headed out to the marina.

She had tried to sit in the stands at the football game first. But it was one of the most miserable things she had ever done, being surrounded by people in such a festive place, forced to smile and exchange pleasantries. She didn't care at all about the new diner that was opening on Main Street or the cold front that had blown through last week or the shoe sale in Osceola at a boutique called Stepping Stones. She couldn't escape the darkness in her heart long enough to listen to anyone or to pretend that she cared.

And underneath it all, she knew that everyone suspected she knew something that she wasn't saying. By now, they had heard about the *Democrat Reflex* and the radio station showing up at the rally. Lydia had the feeling that other people's light-hearted conversations with her were as forced as her own.

With great relief, she left after the third quarter. But arriving home that night was almost as difficult as sitting at the game. Just walking in the door, hanging her pea jacket on the peg, reminded her that this place would now be without Charlie.

Before Charlie, no hint of masculinity could be found in this place. None of the belongings that he'd left scattered around lately because he had known he would always be returning. No man's fishing galoshes to stumble over sideways by the door. No keys and coins or Leatherman pocketknife left in a tangle on the counter. No khaki jackets forgotten, draped across the arm of a chair.

So many of his things seemed to belong here now. Even his Bible, which he'd brought over when they were talking about writing their own wedding vows. Everywhere she looked reminded her of what they'd lost.

Lydia removed the coat from the peg again, shrugged into it, and left. Ten minutes later, in the dark, she parked beside the Viney Creek Marina at Uncle Cy's.

Soft light spilled from what looked like a gas lantern that had been set on the end of the dock. For a moment, as the light flared, it elongated her small shadow and illuminated what was left of the hollyhocks beside the boathouse.

A hot jolt scalded her. *He wouldn't be here, would he?* "Charlie? Is it you?" She took large and hurried steps toward the wooden platform he had built, certain that it was him, that he'd come, that he was waiting here for her. She bolted all the way to the water before she checked herself. She placed her palm against the side of her cheek, laid her face against it, seeking refuge in the cool of her own skin.

She heard the sound of a child laughing. A different man's voice called out, "No, it isn't Charlie."

Unwarranted, ridiculous disappointment plummeted all the way to her toes. "I'm so sorry. I thought—" But of course it wouldn't be him. She didn't want it to be him.

"Lydia? Is that you?"

"Yes."

"Come on out and share the light."

"Who—?"

"It's me."

"Who?"

"Brad Gritton."

"Oh."

There wasn't any way she could gracefully back out of this. And, suddenly, she wasn't certain that she wanted to. She had heard how he had unplugged the sound system this morning. For that, she would be eternally grateful.

Clutching her coat around her in the damp night air, she stepped forward. There, illuminated in the light, sat Brad and a little boy with dark, downy hair that fuzzed like goose down around his face. The back of it swirled in knots and stuck straight out, the ultimate bed head.

"Hey," she said, her voice gone softer when she saw the child.

The little boy, probably about four, hung on to a fishing pole with one hand. Brad held on to it with the other.

"Hi."

"Hi." Then, "You night fishing?"

"Yep. It's way past the kid's bedtime, but I promised. Meet Taylor."

Lydia bent so she could see the boy's face. "I didn't know you—" She stopped.

But Brad was shaking his head. "I don't. He's my sister's."

The little boy sat on the very end of the pier, hunched over in a warm little corduroy coat, staring at the frenzied wisps of fins from the brim drawn to the light. The legs of his flannel pajamas were rolled up to his knees. His feet were wet and bare.

"Hi, Taylor. I'm Lydia. Very nice to meet you."

With eyes as bright as candles, he clutched the cork handle of the pole, his hand tiny and perfect, as pale as moonglow, with his uncle's huge hand right beside it. "Nith to meet you, thoo."

Brad grinned.

"Why aren't you at the game?" she asked.

"Too loud for us over there." Brad rumpled his nephew's hair. "Isn't it, kid?"

"Yeah."

"Yeah," Brad repeated.

After a pause: "This is a good chance," she said, "to thank

you for what you did yesterday. You could have joined right in with the journalism vultures."

His fingers moved through his nephew's hair. "I didn't like their method. There are better ways."

"You did what was right for the kids."

"I did what I believed."

That brought a long string of silence.

Taylor broke it by dabbing his toes in the water again, just for a half a second, and screeching.

Lydia couldn't help having motherly instincts. "You don't think it's too cold for his feet to be in the water out here?"

Brad pulled a towel from his pocket. "We're prepared. I told him his toes looked like worms and, if he wiggled them enough, he might get a fish to bite them."

Silence came again. It was interrupted only by the distant surging of cricket song and the *slap slap slap* of waves breaking against the pilings.

"Hey," he said at last. "Today I learned something about you."

She stiffened, thinking he would say he had learned that she had made the report to Nibarger, that she had protected Shelby and betrayed Charlie. "That so?" She steeled herself.

"They've got all these old issues of the *Democrat Reflex* on microfiche over at the newspaper office. I was running a search and I found something."

"What?"

"That story about you going out when you were young and finding people. About how you were the one who helped find that Boy Scout who got lost."

"Oh, *that.*"

"What was that, Lydia? How did you go out in the woods like that and lead everybody to that kid? How did you know where to find him?"

If she hesitated to answer, her heart was softened by the sight of Brad bringing out the towel again and drying the little boy's feet. "There, now," he whispered to Taylor as he rolled the child's little plaid pajama legs down so they reached his ankles. Next he began to tug on a pair of warm socks. "I think we've had enough fishing for one night, little guy."

"Nowadays," she said, "I can't even find myself."

Out on the Brownbranch, a duck must have gotten disturbed in its sleep. A loud *quack* echoed across the water. For a moment they both stared into the blackness toward the sound. "The story said that, when you were a little girl, you touched the trunks of trees. That people thought trees talked to you. Were they just making all that up?"

She didn't say anything right off. Then, "It was coming here that made it start." Yes, she remembered that. "There's always been something special about Shadrach."

"When it started? What started?"

"Being out in the woods and knowing which way to turn. That's all it was." Then, "It didn't frighten me, you know. I used to think it was God."

"Oh," he said quietly. "God." Taylor's grip had loosened on the fishing pole. His eyelids had gone half mast, his little body rocking from the struggle of keeping his eyes open. Brad rescued the pole and reeled in the line. With thumbnail and forefinger, he peeled the dead worm off the hook and flipped it into the water. "The great paradox of God."

Taylor had slumped over onto Brad's knee. Brad turned the knob on the lantern as the light went low and then flickered out completely. What had looked like a very dark night overhead began to glimmer and shine with stars.

"What do you mean by that?"

"The love in the world. Everybody says it's there. Well, if it is, then it's the most consistent thing in the world. But how can something so consistent also be so unpredictable?"

He took off his own coat and bunched it around Taylor's little body, then lifted the child up and tossed him over his shoulder like a sack of Missouri sorghum. Somehow he found the fishing pole in the dark, and the tackle box, too.

"Here," she said. "I'll carry the lantern."

"Thanks."

They walked the length of the pier together. When their feet began to crunch acorns and they were back on dry land, he told her, "Taylor's mom died of cancer last year. My sister was the best friend I ever had."

"I'm sorry."

"So are a lot of people."

"I don't know what to say."

"It's okay. Nobody does. I don't." Then, "There are things to be grateful for, I suppose. But I just don't get it sometimes. Why God does what He does."

"Now you're the one who's talking about God."

"Yeah."

Lydia stared out into nothingness. "Maybe that's how it used to be for me, too, with the trees. I don't know how to do it anymore. Now maybe it's all just . . . words."

Brad didn't say anything. He didn't ask any questions. And suddenly, despite all of Brad's digging for the answers, maybe because of them, she felt safe to talk.

"The things they asked in that meeting this morning were awful. She had to repeat what had happened over and over again. What made her say someone had acted inappropriately with her? How many times had it happened? Had he forced her to touch him when she didn't want to?"

Yes, Shelby had answered. *It had happened four or five times. Yes, he made me touch him back.*

"She held on to my hand the whole time," Lydia said to Brad, "like I was the only one who could keep her from sinking into quicksand."

"It doesn't get any tougher than that."

"No."

"Wow."

"Taylor's asleep."

"Yeah."

They stopped walking, stood listening to the even, deep breathing of the little boy.

"I really love this kid," Brad said, his voice lowered to a whisper. "We don't get to see each other often, but we're all trying to get things on an even keel again. He lives with his dad in Kentucky."

"Is that what you mean about God being a paradox?" she asked, her voice a whisper, too, because a paradox, when she looked at Brad and his nephew together, seemed like something she wanted to understand.

"I've discovered that you always know where you stand with God; you seldom know what He's going to do next."

The water moved out past the rim of light. She looked at him, shrugged her shoulders, gave a sad little laugh. "All you were doing was fishing with your nephew. And you got me instead."

"That isn't such a bad thing, maybe."

They'd walked all the way to Brad's SUV. She opened the door for him so he could put the little boy inside. "Thanks for letting me talk."

"What you've told me is confidential, Lydia," he said. "I know Charlie Stains is the teacher who cleared out his room today. I know there was a meeting. If I do any story about this, it will be based on my own research, on court records and official statements and police reports."

"For some reason," she said to the stars that seemed to throb and move above the lake, "I already knew that."

One beat passed. Another.

"Would you mind taking my coat off this kid while I hold him?" Gently, he held Taylor out toward her. "That way I'll have something to cushion his head."

"Yes, I will." Lydia smiled a little, the first time she had smiled in three days, as she unwrapped the boy's willowy limbs and folded Brad's heavy green army jacket into a pillow.

CHAPTER TWELVE

The porch light hadn't been left on for him, which wasn't a good sign. Sam mounted the three brick steps to the Olins' house that night and rang the doorbell anyway. As its hollow *ding-dong* echoed somewhere far inside, he heard a distant muffle of conversation, approaching footsteps.

When the light came on, it was the first time he realized Shelby's door had a peephole in it. He saw the convex glass darken, knew that the lens and light were being blocked by somebody's eye.

Sam fiddled with the wallet in his back pocket, which contained thirty-seven dollars in wrinkled, limp bills. He craned his neck at the porch ceiling, whistled a few bars of a song he couldn't remember the name to. In one corner of the cedar siding, a perfect web vibrated as a spider moved in toward a tiny, trapped gnat.

The eye must have left, because Sam saw empty light through the peephole again. Then, as quickly as he'd noticed it missing, the eye came back again. He couldn't figure out what was going on. Why was Shelby acting so strange?

Sam rocked backward onto the heels of his father's Sunday shoes, examining the polished Bordeaux toes. They were the only pair he'd been able to find in the house appropriate for a formal dance. With both hands he lifted, in offering fashion, the clear plastic box with its chrysanthemum corsage and its curled ribbons. He shifted his weight from his right foot to his left. From his left foot to his right. And felt his underarm Sport Speed Stick begin to fail.

Finally, the door cracked open. A yellow cat with a tattered ear shot out, weaving a question mark between his legs. Tom Olin's square frame filled the space. "Hello, Sam."

Sam shifted his weight from his right back to his left again. He started to speak but nothing came out. He cleared his throat. "I'm here to pick up Shelby for the dance."

"I'm sorry," Mr. Olin said. "I thought she would have called you before now. I'm afraid she doesn't want to go."

Sam, his shoulders slumping, just stood there, wondering what he was supposed to say. He gave what felt like a foolish smile and scooped the cat off the ground. The feline dangled over his forearm as if it had no backbone. "Come on, Butterball." Shelby had named the cat after the turkey last Thanksgiving. "You aren't supposed to be outside."

In a fit of wisdom, though, Sam held on to the animal

and handed over the enormous flower instead. Mr. Olin took it cautiously, as if he thought it might give him hay fever.

"Maybe you could give it to her. Maybe she would see it and change her mind."

"I don't think that's going to happen, son."

"I'd like to at least *try*."

A man would have to be dead to resist such a plea. Tom glanced from flower to boy, from boy to flower, and back again. Tom wasn't dead. He stepped back to admit both boy and Butterball. "Here. Got to close this fast. Don't want to let the crazy cat out again."

From the direction of the kitchen Sam heard a rush of faucet water. At the latching of the door, it turned off.

"You did the right thing sending that boy away, Tom," came a woman's voice. "This is something that needs to be handled inside our family."

"Well, dear," the man said, his voice pitched about three notes higher in warning, "while you're circling the wagons, you'd better come say hello to Sam. He's standing right here."

Tamara Olin appeared, drying her wrists on an apron, unable to cover her surprise. "Oh, hello, Sam. Where did you come from?"

Sam's red-and-black diagonal necktie, which he'd also pilfered from deep inside his dad's closet, had begun to chafe. He yanked at the knot, playing it back and forth like the pendulum on the grandfather clock beside the stairs. His ribs ached. He'd loaded up with Vioxx again.

"I come from Mizzura," he said, teasing, trying to erase her awful expression, trying to bring back some hint of a smile to her face.

A smile never came. "You've got to know this is hard, Sam. There are too many sad things happening around here."

"What's hard?"

"I just don't think Shelby's going to be able to go to the dance with you."

Shirt. Shoes. Belt. Trousers. The hardest thing Sam had done in six months was piece together an appropriate outfit for this thing. He hoped that nobody noticed his pants were black and that his jacket was navy blue. Underneath everything else, he was still wearing his favorite white athletic socks.

"If you'd just let me talk to her," Sam said. "I know she isn't sick or anything. She was at the game. I saw her."

Shelby's mom untied her apron strings in sharp little tugs. She laid it aside and her hands folded in on each other. "Some things are *helpless*. Some things, you just can't change."

Mr. Olin didn't invite Sam to join him when he settled in on the couch. Instead he sifted page by page through real-estate listings, which Sam read upside down. EXPANSIVE LIVING ROOM, JUST REMODELED, BROWNBRANCH VIEWS, SELF-CONTAINED RV PAD. "For Pete's sake, let the kid off the hook, Tamara. We are in control of this thing. We know the legal steps we need to take. We will make happen what needs to happen. Nothing's going to be helped by keeping her locked up in this house like a criminal."

"I just can't send her out into the world right now, Tom."

"Look, I'm not telling you this isn't a desperate situation. But I think you're making it worse."

"She's my *daughter*."

"You're the one she needs to remind her that she's worth something, that she's still the same."

"So help me, Tom, she'll never be the same. She's been *ruined*."

As if the woman's words were meant as introduction instead of lament, Shelby's figure, waiflike, appeared at the head of the stairs. "Sa-am?"

"Shelb." He raced to the middle of the room where she could see him.

"I'm so sorry about all of this."

"About what?"

"I-I can't go."

"Of course you can go. I'm here to pick you up. It's *homecoming*."

"I can't help it."

"Give me one reason why."

"It's better if you do this without me."

"No, it isn't."

"You know how much fun you have when you hang

out with everybody else. You'll get to dance with all your friends."

"Why would I want to dance with anybody else, Shelb?"

"You just *should*."

"You tell me *why*."

"I just. I'm not . . . maybe you need to find somebody who isn't me, Sam." She stood clutching the rail, staring down at her fingers. "There's reasons I'm just not . . . a person you should be *interested in* anymore."

"Is it me?" he asked.

She didn't answer.

Seeing his number painted on her cheek had made him brave. "You tell me this one thing," he pushed. "Are you trying to get rid of me?"

Tears glimmered in her eyes. She shook her head. Said quietly, "No."

"Well, then—"

She stood over him, leaning, looking as if she wanted to hand him her whole soul with her eyes.

"There isn't anything you can do to make me feel anything different about you than I already feel."

"You don't know that, Sam. We're just *kids*."

Shelby's mother flicked a rag over the surfaces of things on the shelves. The woman's shoulders lifted and fell as if she were grieving for some dying friend. "I just don't think we need to face anybody with this yet."

"Mama—"

141

The dust rag wafted over a row of books, all sizes and shapes of them, some leather-bound, some trade paperback, some gold-leaved. "You know I invited Grandpa to have dinner with us tonight. I thought having a family-time together might help. It's your favorite, Sauce Pot Meatballs." She began to arrange the books one by one on the shelf. She made certain each spine stood flush with the one to its right and to its left. The volumes aligned perfectly, like soldiers, their dustcovers smooth and straight.

"Shelb—" Sam tried.

But at last her stepfather slapped down his real-estate Multiple Listing book and leapt up from the couch. "She can't hide away forever, Tammy. If you ask me, this young lady is very brave and smart, doing everything she's done. I'd like to see you give her some credit for that."

Tamara stopped working and stared at him. She stood gripping one hand with the other as if she had to struggle not to cry.

Shelby leaned farther over the railing as the cat loped up the carpeted stairs on weightless paws.

And Tom propped up the cushions on the couch, obviously something his wife had spoken to him about in the past. The sofa looked like he hadn't been sitting there at all.

"Pumpkin, I have to say I agree with Sam. You ought to go have a good time and forget about everything else for a little while."

"*Thomas.* She's my daughter, not yours. How can you usurp me like this?"

But Tom winked at Sam. Tom lifted his palms in acceptance toward Shelby. "I saw you carrying in that pretty dress from the mall in Springfield last week. It would be a shame not to get the chance to wear it."

CHAPTER THIRTEEN

───── ❦ ─────

*R*olls of black paper plastered the doors at the school to block out the fluorescent lights. As dance-goers entered the gym through a confusing maze of room dividers and disco balls, strobe lights made it look like they were walking in jerks, illuminating them as if they were clicking through the frames of a disjointed black-and-white movie.

A makeshift stage had been set up at one end of the gym and on that platform a small-town disc jockey reigned, gigantic speakers and amplifiers heaped around him like moving boxes, giggling girls shouting requests and, like groupies, hanging on to his every word. Lightning-bolt letters sizzled along one side of an amp. VOLTSTAR PRODUCTIONS, they announced. BOOK VOLTSTAR FOR YOUR ST. CLAIR COUNTY WEDDINGS, BAR MITZVAHS AND BARBECUES.

"Hey, Sam. *Buddy*." A variety of high fives all around. "About time you showed up."

"Hey, Shelb. That's a nice dress."

"Thanks. Hi, Will. Hey, Tommy."

Friends crowded up around them and Sam had the claustrophobic feeling, all of a sudden, of being encroached upon by a wolf pack. "So, what took you guys so long to get here?"

"Yeah, where you been?"

Sam's eyes met Shelby's. "We took our time, that's all."

"People are starting to wonder what Shelby looks like. She missed all the royalty introductions again."

"How come you're being so quiet, Shelby?"

Shelby, who'd been walking right beside Sam, grabbed the collar of his shirt hard enough for him to feel her short fingernails. "Let's just dance, okay? Let's don't talk to anybody for a while."

"Okay."

Sam was torn between worrying about her and thinking how amazing she looked. She hadn't put on any perfume, but she smelled like clean itself—earth and air, with just a hint of lemon that must have been her shampoo. When she stepped out in front of him, the sight of her white dress billowing from the small of her waist like a lily bloom, the way her hair swung long against her bare shoulders tonight (she almost always wore it up in a comb with sunglasses on top at school)—all of this made him slightly dizzy.

They'd walked in to a slow dance with a strong beat. He

held his arms out to her, expecting her to move into them. "Watch out," Will bellowed. "Things are going to get hot in here now!"

Tommy Ballard came down to the end of the chairs to watch. "You *go,* Leavitt. You *go.*"

"*You* go," Sam hollered back at them. "You go and dance with your *own* girls."

So much was going on that he was the only one who noticed it—how Shelby hesitated, queerly distant, as if suddenly she wasn't certain whether she should touch him or not.

"Come on," he whispered. "It's okay."

"I don't want to hurt your ribs."

"I've been playing football, Shelby. I don't think there's any more damage *you* could do."

The music changed. One minute they were in the twenty-first century and the next, "The Hokey Pokey." A yell went up in the crowd as everybody put their right arms in, out, shook them all about. Shelby jumped into the dance as if it were the most important musical performance she'd ever participated in. Sam narrowed his eyes in concern, began to go through the motions beside her.

∽

OF COURSE, NONE of the girls at the dance would go to the ladies' room by themselves.

As the night wore on and the females of Shadrach High School began to rove and disappear in larger and larger numbers, the young men had their usual speculations:

somebody's zipper had split. Somebody's chignon had sprung loose and needed fourteen more bobby pins. Somebody needed to borrow a tube of mascara.

Tommy Ballard was the one who noticed it first. Perhaps it was because Sam had told him he had to find his own girl to dance with. Perhaps it was because Tommy kept a large and rather outlandish hickory slingshot stuck in the rear pocket of his dress pants and whenever he saw an interesting prospect without an escort tagging along, he grabbed a handful of ice from the cafeteria ice machine and let it fly.

"Man," he whispered when he managed to grab his best friend's elbow and drag him over. "Sam, something's really bogus."

"What?"

"There are no females around. They all took off."

"What do you mean, they all took off?"

"Take a look at this room. Who do you see?"

"A bunch of guys."

"Yeah."

"Well, the ladies have to be *somewhere*. Definitely a serious lack of potential candidates in this room. Furthermore," Tommy pulled out his slingshot and scraped it across the edge of his sleeve, "I guess you haven't noticed Shelby's friends. Do you realize that not one of them has come to talk to her since the two of you walked in?"

"Say, Tommy," and Sam had in mind telling him something sarcastic like, *Butt out, Ballard. This isn't your life; it's mine.* But just as he opened his mouth to say it, he swallowed his words. When he thought about it, Tommy was right. And now, all those girls Tommy had been missing were purposefully marching right toward them through paper-covered double doors, through the strobe lights, across the dance floor lit by jewel flashes from the overhead disco balls.

Whitney Allen raised her hands, her mouth smirking. That's when Sam's stomach pitched—when he saw her fake smile, her dark, intent eyes.

"Hey, Whit." He tried to head her off. "How you doing?"

She ignored his question. This was a bad sign. She made a megaphone out of her fingers and called over the music, "Shelby, hi."

Shelby turned, gave an innocuous smile. "Hi."

"Wanted to come over and tell you something." The words in a neutral tone, not humble, not haughty. For a moment, when she said this, Sam felt a sense of relief. "I thought you had a great soccer game last Friday."

"Thanks."

Nothing to worry about, he thought. *Just soccer. Just things girls always talk about when they disappear with each other.*

In the small of his back, he could feel Tommy poking him hard with the two prongs of his slingshot. The jabbing sensation seemed far away. The strobe lights pulsed, savage and fast, connecting to a throbbing hurt behind his eyes.

"I *really* wish I could play games the way you do." Whitney's head was down, her face suddenly hidden, and Sam's sense of relief started to slip away.

"You can. You're a good player, Whitney."

"Are your parents going over to the Fremont game next week?"

"Yeah, I guess. I—I mean, I think they will."

"Well, I don't see why they'd come, because you're not going to play. My dad says they'll kick you off the team because of all the lies you've told."

Sam looked up. Shelby's fingers bore down, her nails cutting into the back of his hand. His belly swarmed with alarm, as if he'd been caught in something he couldn't understand, like a bewildered child who only knows that he's in the middle of something bad.

Shelby, leaning against his left arm, pushing him forward as if he were the only thing standing between her and a deadly fall. Her voice was calm, firm, unafraid. "I don't know what you're talking about."

"Ha. I think you do. The newspaper reporter who snuck into the pep assembly yesterday."

It seemed impossible that she had missed all of that, he thought. Impossible that she'd been somewhere else in the building and hadn't seen the disturbance the *Democrat Reflex* had caused.

Sam heard the little, sarcastic bite rising in Whitney's voice, didn't like it, couldn't stop it. "We know he asked all those questions because of you. You're the one who made all those accusations."

Shelby didn't move. Sam could feel her breath when she inhaled and didn't let it go. The blinking strobe lights, their cruel pulse somewhere deep behind his temples. And he couldn't stop himself. He had to ask it.

Because he needed to know, too.

"Shelby, is that really true?"

"I don't know anything about that. I don't know anything about the pep assembly. I wasn't there."

"I know," Sam said. "But where were you?"

Whitney's teeth stood out like milk glass beneath the stain of *Mocha Mousse* lip gloss. "Does Sam know what you've been doing? Does he know what happened with Mr. Stains?"

Sam felt Shelby working her way out of his grasp as if he were the one she needed to escape from. "Shelb?"

"You could have done anything else to get attention," Whitney said. "Why did you have to screw things up for *him?*"

He wanted to hold Shelby against him, to keep her safe from them. He wanted them to be wrong. "What is it, Shelb? What are they talking about?"

Tears glimmered in her eyes as she backed away. "Don't ask me, Sam. Please don't ask me."

"Shelb. I'm here, don't you see? I'm just trying to help you."

"Well, you can't."

"Maybe you owe me."

"I don't owe you anything. I don't have to respond to any of this if I don't want to. That's what they said."

Whitney lifted her chin like a hound on the scent. "Who said that? The cops said that? Is that what they told you when you reported Mr. Stains?"

"Shelby." From somewhere in the distance, Sam heard the sound of his own suspicious voice. "Did something happen between you and him?"

"No," she cried, "Oh, no."

"Then, what?"

"Not like what you're thinking."

"Then what's everybody talking about it for?" Adrenaline surged up his spine. "Are you the student they were talking about at the assembly yesterday?"

Of course he had known something was wrong, with the way her mother had gone on and her stepdad had peered out of the peephole and the way she'd had to be coaxed into her dress.

But in sort of a naïve, superhuman way, he had thought nothing could have gone wrong for Shelby that his caring about her couldn't fix. In his wildest dreams, he couldn't have imagined this.

If that teacher's done something to her, I'll kill him.

Questions dropped on them, raining down from every direction, sifting groundward, as if they were standing in the woods and leaves had begun to fall.

"What exactly did he do to you, Shelby? What was so bad that you had to run to everybody and blab?"

"You must feel guilty, don't you?"

Sam scooped his arm around her waist, tried to propel her out of the crowd. And mouthed, *Come on, Shelb. I'll take you home.*

"Remember last week when you told me he was your favorite teacher, Shelb? I do."

"How's he your favorite teacher if, the next week, you say something that ruins his life?"

"I don't want to go home," she said, wresting away from Sam. "I'd rather die than go back to that place right now."

"You'll be safest—"

The voices around them shrill and hostile, "But Mr. Stains will never be safe. You made him lose his job."

Whitney's white hand lifted like a chalice above their heads, as if she could reach beyond everyone's questions and string them together to her liking. "Shelby, you can't leave the dance without this."

"Without what?"

"Your crown."

"Why don't you get that later?" Sam asked, a little angry at Shelby now, and frightened because of it. "Let's get out of here. Somebody else can pick it up, okay?"

He tried to steer Shelby away, applying pressure against her spine, against that vulnerable, beautiful curve that he loved, where white chiffon and zipper and gathers met. There was a general rustle of skirts, some cautious, jittery laughter, a hush of ugly expectation. Up it came, passed from hand to hand, as the dancers split or moved tightly together to let the thing pass through.

"Here you go," somebody said, and Sam heard her gasp. Her eyes had adjusted to the blinking dark-and-light faster than his own, but he saw it a moment later. He saw the thing staring out over them like a round, inflated head. It wore a rhinestone crown. Someone had given it eyes, a nose, a hackneyed, thin grin.

It's just the stupid soccer ball, he lectured himself. *They got it out of her house or something.*

Hand-sewn, it said. Gyro KwikGoal. Shelby's ball.

The face had probably been drawn with a Sharpie, or something else that would never wash off. The eyes were big and weepy, the upturned nose drawn like a pig's nose.

"That's mine." Shelby grabbed the ball from Whitney, locking it away beneath her arm. "Where did you get this?"

"I don't know," Whitney said. "It just showed up."

A roomful of people exchanged blank stares. Not a one of them seemed to know anything more than that. Not one girlfriend stepped forward to stand beside Shelby or to support her. Sam knew that, since they'd started dating, she had cut herself off from most of them. And from somewhere in another world, the strobes were still pounding, Voltstar Productions was still churning out dance party songs.

"This is for the girls who love to make *noise*," the deejay shouted, his mouth jammed up sideways against the microphone. Drums picked up the rhythm and music swelled. *Who let the dogs out? Uh-oh-oh-oh?*

Sam could see the curse words that they'd scribbled across the leather, to accompany their pictures, written in bold, dashy strokes.

LIAR.

LIAR.

LIAR.

Shelby yanked off the tiara they'd taped on it and pitched it across the floor. It didn't take more than a moment for the thing to be broken beneath someone's feet.

"You'll get ink on your dress," Sam urged her. "Give me the ball, Shelby. Please just let me carry it for you."

"No," she said, clutching it, refusing to let it go. "I can carry it by myself." With defiance, she tucked it tighter inside the crook of her elbow.

CHAPTER FOURTEEN

———— ✌ ————

The storm began as a black stain against the stars to the east, the underbellies of the clouds lit by the street-light on the corner of Montgomery and Elbow Knob that stayed burning all night long.

First came the dry rasp of leaves across rooftops, the soft scudding as the wind lifted leaves from the ground, swirling them in the corners between houses. Lydia heard the rain begin just after midnight, while she lay in bed knowing she wouldn't sleep—those first few drops that smacked the pavement and left a wet spot the size of your thumb.

Lydia's nose burned with unshed tears. And every time she closed her eyes, she envisioned sheets of water like sheets of grief, falling the way they fell into the Brownbranch when a storm was windy and pouring, like ruffles on the hem of a petticoat surging across the ground.

She closed her eyes. This time, as she struggled to pray, words finally came into her mind.

No tears. Please God, no tears.

And even as she thought it, she wiped her face with the back of her hand and found it wet.

The rain spattered off awnings and poured out of gutters like someone had turned on a spigot. It ran down the glass panes and splashed on the shingles and sang its way in rivulets down the eaves.

I know I'm supposed to believe in Charlie. But all I feel is punished.

And somewhere beyond the clatter of the autumn storm, Lydia almost thought she heard tapping at the door.

Father, why would You let adolescent girls have to know the things Shelby knows?

She rolled to her other side, punched up the feather pillow that had seen better days, closed her eyes.

Why would You let broken lives be the picture of your love?

Her eyes opened. *Tap tap tap. Tap tap tap.*

She listened for the wind, realized it had passed. Only the rain made any sound, and that had settled to a tender soak. She heard the knocking again.

Off went the covers. With a blind hand and a huge clatter, she felt around for her cotton robe, knocking a stack of magazines and her massive bottle of women's vitamins off the top of her nightstand. The lampshade jostled. She finally found the robe, sailed it across her shoulders, shoved an arm into each sleeve. She made her way downstairs on cold, bare toes, letting each step groan with her weight before she moved on to the next one.

When she peered out the oval, beveled glass, everything looked rain-streaked, a mercury gray. But on the porch she could see the small, hunched form, the watercolor smudge of something white. A young woman. A child.

"Shelby."

She couldn't get the lock opened fast enough. She flung the door open to the fresh ozone smell of rain. And to the girl who, like a cat, looked smaller because she was drenched.

Water plastered Shelby's blonde hair in strings to her head. Her dress clung to her small thighs, to the athletic shapes of her legs, the knobs of her knees. Water sheeted her lips and dripped off her chin. Her mouth was trembling, almost blue. Lydia threw open the screen and guided her by the elbow. The robe came off Lydia's shoulders and went around Shelby almost before the girl could be ushered inside the door.

"Come into the den," Lydia said. "Get yourself dried off. There are coals. It won't take a minute to open the damper and warm up the house."

Shelby nodded without saying anything. She stepped forward with frozen, small, shuffling steps, her teeth chattering.

"I'm getting towels," Lydia said, still directing her toward the stove. "You stand right there."

With everything else going on, Lydia hadn't done laundry in a week. In the bathroom, she pulled towels from the hamper and shook them out one by one. She found one or two that seemed useable and dry. As an afterthought, she grabbed an old nightgown, too, thinking it might be best to coax the girl out of her wet clothing.

I believe this is my job, Lord, but how many times do You want me to stand beside this child? No matter how much it hurts, why do You keep sending her to me again?

Shelby stood where Lydia had left her, huddled beside the Vermont Castings stove where the coals made red, roving patterns in the ash, like hidden threads of silk. "Let's get you out of that wet stuff, okay?"

"T-this is m-my new dress," Shelby whimpered.

Lydia peeled the robe off Shelby's shoulders as Shelby shuddered with cold. Chills racked the girl's arms. The chiffon dress was not only wet; the skirt had been torn. Mud plastered her bare legs. She must have been running for miles through the brambles.

Shelby was shivering violently when Lydia saw the horrid thing knotted in her elbows against her body.

"What's this?"

Lydia held out a hand for the soccer ball.

For a long moment Shelby just shook her head at Lydia, shuddering. Then, even then, she really didn't let the thing go. She just loosened her arms around it and the ball rolled out, bouncing onto the floor.

Lydia watched it roll away, reading it all the way until it bobbed against the trim in the corner.

"I'm sorry," she said. "Oh, honey. I'm so sorry."

She cupped Shelby's purple fingers inside her own and blew.

Shelby leaned in, touching her wet head to Lydia's.

"I j-just feel so ashamed." Her first words since stumbling inside the door. "I c-can't make it stop. People are l-looking at me and . . . and thinking. And if they're not thinking about what I've done, then they're thinking that I'm a liar."

Lydia began to towel Shelby off, her face gone taut with anger. She tousled Shelby's hair. She rubbed hard, as if she was trying to remove something that was much worse than water.

"H-He was my favorite teacher. I don't know why I—" She lifted her face. "There isn't anybody who can help me, Miss P." Shelby's shoulders rose and fell.

The embers in the grate had caught fire again. Once she'd finished toweling the girl off, Lydia slipped in a few extra lengths of hickory and adjusted the flue. She held up the nightgown. "You can put this on." And got the first smile she'd gotten out of Shelby since she'd walked in the door.

"You want me to wear that?"

"You can be fashion conscious if you want to," with a lift of her eyebrows. "But it's dry."

The girl peeled off the straps of her dress while the fire played blue-golden on her skin. Then she stopped, blushing with modesty, her arms crossed over the loose bodice of the dress.

"Oh, Shelby. I'm sorry. I hadn't even thought—" Lydia handed over the huge wad of flannel. "There's a guest bedroom where you can change in here. Bathroom's that door on the right. Put your dress on a hanger over the bathtub where it can drip."

That age, Lydia thought, *where one minute they're ready to take on the world and the next they're terrified by it.*

When Shelby returned, she'd wrapped her wet hair into a towel turban. The nightgown enveloped her, dry and warm. She stood in front of the stove, which was kicking out breakers of heat, while tiny glints of fire reflected in her eyes.

"You going to be okay?"

She was still buttoning, settling into the flannel the way she would settle into a hug. "Yeah."

"Good." A little smile of satisfaction, shared between them. Then Lydia asked, "Shelby, does your family know where you are?"

The girl shook her head no.

"How did you get all the way over here?"

"I ran."

"Where did you run from?"

"From Sam. From the dance. After they did this—" she nodded toward the soccer ball. "Now I know what everybody thinks."

She told Lydia how she'd burst away from Sam as he'd

tried to lead her away from the kids who were taunting her, how she'd sprinted through the woods. She told how she hadn't been able to lose him until she'd stashed the ball inside the fork of a sycamore and climbed up into the tree.

"And, does Sam think you're a liar, too?"

"He wants me to be lying. I can see it in his eyes."

As new hickory began to zing and hiss in the woodstove and cocoa began to warm on the burner in the kitchen, a gentle silence overtook them. Their two sadnesses, once separate, churned and mingled.

Oh, Lord. Where are You when You feel this far away? Where are You when it hurts like this?

Lydia could smell cocoa scorching in the pan. She stood and asked, "You want marshmallows in your hot chocolate?"

"Oh, yes. Please."

Lydia poured the hot drinks, stirring each mug with a careful twirl. She didn't know where this awful feeling of shame was coming from as she stood there in the kitchen, the spoon handle turning warm in her hand. It was as if something inside herself had suddenly grown too heavy to bear.

If You are there, Lord, how could You allow something to happen that would let a guiltless girl feel shame?

Lydia opened the bag of marshmallows and pitched a handful into each cup.

Why won't You take this away? You know it's something I never wanted to walk through.

"I'm going to call your parents, Shelby," she said when she walked back into the den. "I'll tell them you're safe here and that I'll bring you home. I don't want them to worry." The spoons clattered when she set everything on the coffee table. Lydia took a quick sip of hers, gulped hard because it was hot. "I'll also tell them to call Sam and let him know you're okay."

"Thank you," Shelby said. "That'll be good."

Lydia didn't have to look up the Olins' number. She had called it so many times during this past week that she had it memorized. After she'd spoken with them, she returned to the sofa and sat down.

"What's this thing?" Shelby held up a clothbound book with the embossed etching of a tiger surrounded by stars. THE LICHEN BRIDGE PECK-N-PAW it said in silver leaf across the bottom.

"Oh, that?" Lydia gave a light laugh of dismissal. "My high school yearbook."

Before Lydia could stop her, Shelby started snooping through. "Are you in here?"

"No." Lydia shrugged it off. "Well, sort of. Maybe in one or two places." And no need for anybody to find the right pages, either. "Nothing big."

"Were you popular?"

"No."

Shelby smiled for the second time tonight.

"Why does that matter? Why are you smiling?"

"Because you keep saying no to everything. I guess you just wanted to look at yourself when you were young!"

"Oh."

Shelby spooned a pile of melted marshmallow into her mouth. And Lydia decided Shelby's smile had been enough of a treasure that she could let her guard down a little.

"I was looking at it because of homecoming," Lydia offered. "When you kids celebrate yours, it makes me think about mine again, too." She touched the girl's shoulder. "I was thinking of the times I've gone back home since I moved here. Did you know I was even planning a trip back there during the Christmas holidays? But I don't think I'm going now."

Shelby kept thumbing through the pages. She held it high in both hands and raised her voice to read aloud. "'To one of the nicest chicks I've ever met.'" A sidelong grin. "Ha! He called you a chick, Miss P. Who is this? Was he cute?"

"None of your business. Give that back." But when Lydia tried to swipe it away, Shelby giggled and lifted it higher.

"'Never forget Mrs. Bodkin's French class and the FOOT patrol and the way Mr. Johnson made meatloaf in the Petrie dish and the famous noise like a rhino. I STILL think you were the best lab partner. Remember, never eat Johnson's meatloaf! I know you will go far in life (especially with the rhino noise). Call me when you visit Northwestern, Stay sweet and good-looking, Gary.'"

"There. Now you've read my yearbook. Are you happy?"

"I want to hear the noise like a rhino."

"Well, you can keep wanting it, because that's something you'll *never* hear."

On page 21, Shelby found the Future Scientists Club page and, beside a picture of a hanging skeleton someone had written, "Mr. Jarrett after he loses 300 pounds." They giggled at a bonfire picture with a wiener caught in midair where someone had circled the wiener and noted, "The mysterious and profound floating hot dog of LBHS." In the back of the book, in the advertising section, someone had turned a milk carton that read "In Horn's Dairy There Is Strength," into a milk carton that read "In Lichen Bridge There Is Nothing."

Shelby's hair was still up in its turban, but her tormented expression was gone. "Oh, here's another one. Listen. 'Lyd, your friendship has always meant so much to me, especially because you're always willing to listen to me whenever I need advice, and boy have I needed it a lot this year! Especially at 3 a.m., remember?!? Not many people would have done that! It means a lot to me and I will remember it always. I'm not going to tell you to be good because that's hopeless! Have a great summer, Sarah A.'"

Shelby pulled the towel down out of her hair and shook

her head. "That's cool what that one wrote. About how you listen to her."

"Thanks."

"Where are you in here, Miss P?"

Lydia flipped a few pages and pointed out her photo.

"That's you? No way."

"Way."

"Why's your hair all big and poofy like that?"

"Because that was the style back in the dark ages of the eighties."

"It looks like it was curled by a steam roller."

"Steam rollers," Lydia said. "Yes, we used those."

"No, a steam roller. The kind they use to build new roads."

"I am a staff member at your high school," Lydia said. "Your high school counselor. You can't talk about my hair that way."

"Sorry." With a lovely giggle, Shelby smacked the book shut and handed it over. Lydia poked it as far back as it would go on the shelf.

"You know that one thing that girl wrote?" Shelby asked.

"Which one?"

"About how you were always willing to listen?"

"Yeah."

Lydia heard a car drive up outside. She peered out the curtain. "There's an old white Pontiac at the curb. Who is that, Shelb? Is that somebody in your family?"

"My grandfather," Shelby said as she circled her mug rim with one slow finger. "He must have volunteered to come pick me up."

"That's good, isn't it?"

But Shelby only said, "I feel the same way about you as that girl in your yearbook did, Miss P. Whatever happens about anything, I just wanted you to know."

CHAPTER FIFTEEN

———— ✒ ————

*S*unday morning at Big Tree Baptist Church was a morning for wearing Ray-Ban sunglasses. But Lydia was having a difficult time finding hers.

She grabbed for her purse and dug around in it. They weren't there. She scrabbled around on the car seat, checking the cracks and the drink holder. They weren't there, either.

Just then, she remembered she'd been wearing them while she'd been driving. She checked the top of her head with her hand, and there they were. She pulled them down over her eyes and glanced around, hoping that no one had seen that.

The sun was so bright that wet quartz gravel shimmered like opal underfoot. All things nearby and in the distance below them shone with the same radiant, holy brilliance as a candle's glow. Lydia shut her driver-side door and stood with her fingers on the car mirror.

Elbow Knob, where the church stood, marked the highest point in St. Clair County. The view was beautiful all around it.

Lydia removed her sunglasses once more, and buffed the lenses against her shirt hem. As quickly as she'd taken them off, she shoved them onto her nose again, as if hiding behind dark shades might well be the survival tactic of the day.

The Reverend Joe R. Douglas, a long-time fishing buddy of her Uncle Cy's, came billowing across the parking lot in his black chasuble. "Lydia, how are you this morning?"

"I'm fine." What a great liar she was.

He must have caught her taking cover and knew exactly what that meant. "I read the article in the *Democrat Reflex* yesterday. You are involved in all this, aren't you?"

"I'm usually involved when a high school student needs help. It's my job." Then, "There was an article in the newspaper?"

"Yes, very brief and full of facts. There was a police report. It included an official school statement, that an investigation had gotten underway. That was all."

"I see." *Brad did what he said he'd do.*

"You know, of course, that it's everybody else in town who has been filling in the blanks. Charlie Stains, just days after he bought our boat. It's such a shame."

She didn't know whether he meant it was a shame that

Charlie was being held responsible, or it was a shame that somebody responsible had bought the church's boat.

"Charlie always wanted—" Lydia stopped. Of course, she changed the subject. "You always come this far out into the parking lot to greet bystanders, Pastor Joe?"

He gave a little grin and pantomimed the motion of setting a fishhook in a big crappie. "Only if I know somebody's had a tough week. Only if I'm not sure they're going to make it to the door."

The church door had been thrown open to greet the sun. Organ music, in what Lydia recognized as the somewhat questionable but enthusiastic style of Dr. Duncan Minor, vibrated the sumac plumes in the brass umbrella stand that propped open the door. Even all the way out here, you could hear Dr. Minor playing interlude hymns with the same relish as the theme song to *Rollerball*.

In the lull between each new verse of song, snatches of conversation wafted toward them as churchgoers passed the parking lot. ". . . rumors flying . . . no charges . . . investigation . . . that's what I heard . . . there could even be a trial."

"A trial in St. Clair County?"

"Right in that front courthouse room in Osceola, over there where you have to go get your vehicle licenses paid."

For the moment, as Pastor Joe moved on to speak with someone else, Lydia held back. Until this moment on Elbow Knob, with the bright world gleaming in 360 degrees around her, she had not been able to see the full view of her resentment toward God. On the outdoor sign where Joe pasted weekly Scripture readings, it read: He will be like a tree planted by the water that sends out its roots by the stream. It does not fear when heat comes; its leaves are always green.

Okay, so I'm not that tree in the Bible. My limbs are broken and dry. My roots have been ripped up out of the mud. I'm ready to be crushed by the current. Okay.

Regret, as strong as a Missouri king snake, coiled tight around her middle. And, for some reason, Eddy Sandlin came to mind, the story Brad had found on microfiche, the little lost boy she'd found, sitting in the middle of a rushing creek atop a dead snag-wood tree.

I don't know how to get from where I am to where I was. I don't know how to escape from this dry place.

Inside the church's foyer a stainless-steel coffeepot crouched on a table beside Styrofoam cups. A tall spray of red carnations and baby's breath and leather-leaf fern, as widespread as a ballerina's arms, decorated the table. The place smelled like Starbuck's in Springfield and sounded every bit as lively. No, take that back. With the pounding of the organ, it reminded Lydia more of Busch Stadium before a Cardinals game.

"Excuse me, ma'am?" someone asked as she stepped forward, looking for the right place to sit. "Do you mind moving as close toward the front of the sanctuary as possible? And moving toward the center of the row?"

"No. No, that's fine," she said, feeling dismayed. She had hoped to hide in the back.

"Forgive us for moving everybody forward. We're expecting a large crowd today."

Blindly she found herself a space and sat. Her knees bonked the wooden pew box when she did, which jostled a row of Baptist hymnals, a stack of welcome cards, and a multitude of those short, stubby yellow pencils that plunked on the floor and rolled everywhere. She waved at Uncle Cy and Jane across the way. She settled herself, yanking her skirt straight so it covered her stockings, glancing around as if she couldn't figure out who on earth had dropped all those pencils.

Lydia couldn't help overhearing the whispered conversation of the two little ladies on her left. "Can you move over, Trudy? It's so tight in here, I'm having trouble reaching my pocketbook."

"Pastor Joe wouldn't like that one bit."

"It's homecoming weekend. We don't have enough seats for all these extra people."

"Well, I don't like it one bit. I always sit in the second pew over there."

"I know. Somebody's sitting in my place too."

"It's more than that and you know it. You read the newspaper this morning. Small town, big trauma. Everybody heads to the nearest pew."

Lydia glanced up and saw Charlie walking up the aisle toward her. She knew he saw her, too, before her eyes dodged away. She turned forward again, waiting for him, her hand on the pew, her heart pounding.

As he came close, her gaze rose to him. Charlie was very tall. The broad shoulders of his dress suit, his pendulous tie, the questions in his eyes, loomed over her head.

The crisp October morning striking in through the open door, the smell of cured grass and sweet leaves, and the immense crash of the organ playing "Blessed Assurance, Jesus Is Mine!" The entire town was watching. And you can never plan the things you'll say.

Her words rushed out before either of them had the chance to fling up walls. Before either of them had the chance to measure what they'd said before, what they'd thought, how they'd hurt each other.

"How are you?" her heart rushing forward with her words. "How are you holding out?"

"What about you, Lyddie?"

In the few odd seconds while they stared at each other, neither of them realized they had only asked questions, they hadn't answered them.

Over the scent of the wax-polished pews, Lydia could smell mint, soap, cool skin, a Luden's cough drop. "I didn't know you were coming today, Charlie." She cringed at her own voice. She made it sound like she was questioning whether he belonged.

He moved the Luden's from one side of his mouth to the other. She saw his tongue, dyed cough-drop orange. She saw his eyes go dark against her question that spoke of blame. But all of her questions, all of her thoughts, spoke of blame these days. The pain surged between them like an electrical charge. "The new boat," he said, and maybe he was partially honest about this or maybe he wasn't. "I needed to be here today to thank somebody for the boat."

"Oh."

He began to finger his tie. "Lydia?" And the entire length of his sentence, she fought herself to keep from shaking her head. *No. No. Don't ask it, Charlie. Please.*

"You can't sit here," she said, stopping him. "I promised I'd sit with Shelby."

Embarrassed, he looked around the sanctuary over her head, fast, as if he realized he had no right to be with her. She reached to touch his coat sleeve but he jerked it away. She wanted to cry out to him, but she couldn't. *This isn't the place where anyone ought to be taking any stands.*

"I'm sorry." And words alone could never have said how sorry she was.

Charlie had friends who were gesturing to him from the opposite row. *Come over and sit with us.* Patting the seat to make him feel welcome.

"I'll just—" He clapped one fist awkwardly against his hand, snapped his fingers. He backed up, pointed in his friend's general vicinity. "I guess I'll just sit over there."

The choir had begun to file in. The conversations, which moments ago had been buzzing around her, stopped. Suddenly Lydia had room to breathe. Since Charlie had paused to speak to her, it seemed that everyone else had scooted three inches away.

At the front of the sanctuary, the choir members began to sing "Holy, Holy, Holy" with lifted voices and outspread hands. During the entire length of their Call To Worship, Lydia didn't hear any of the words to the song at all. She was only aware of the man who sat four rows in front of her and to the right, his hair barely touching his shirt collar, his shoulders held self-consciously square. She watched until he stood suddenly to speak to an usher. She jerked her attention to the creases in her hand.

Charlie must have forgotten to pick up a church bulletin in the foyer. When he stepped out to get one, he came face to face with Tom and Tamara Olin, who were entering with Shelby.

Tamara gasped and yanked Shelby low against her chest, covering her child's head with her arms.

Tom Olin wrenched sideways, wagging his finger. "You! How could *you* be in a church today? After what you've done to my stepdaughter?"

His voice measured, Charlie said, "I did not do what she says I did."

"Tom." Tamara gripped his arm. "Stop. Don't do this here."

"I ought to haul off and punch you out right now."

"Charlie." Somebody gripped him by the arm. "The service has started."

"Tom," one of the deacons said, "this isn't going to do any good."

Someone pulled Charlie down.

Someone pulled Tom down.

Probably a hundred and twenty-some-odd hearts were pounding as Shelby searched the pews for her counselor and plastered herself against Lydia's side.

After that, Charlie sat still as a post. The tops of his ears, which curled over like the tops of snapdragon blossoms, flushed bright red. Once, he reached to scratch the nape of his neck between his hair and his shirt collar. A thin, oblong slash of sun fell across his shoulders like a bandage.

Lydia made herself turn away.

The Brownbranch glinted toward the east in the view out the window. The only thing that stretched further and fiercer than the sky was the emptiness inside her soul.

The sermon passed in a blur. When she noticed Pastor Joe kept glancing in her direction, Lydia edged the other way, out of his line of sight. Still the pastor's voice boomed toward her, quoting words that she might have once believed, that she might have once clung to.

And, in spite of the heated sermon, the powerful words, the promise of courage, churchgoers' whispers came in quick succession behind her. ". . . Mathis isn't in his usual place . . . neither is Mo Eden's family . . . how about the Bakers? . . . What are you doing sitting over here?"

Be quiet, she wanted to cry out. *Can't you just listen and not care so much about everybody else's business?*

". . . isn't like a wedding where you sit behind the bride or the groom . . . of course it isn't . . . much more important than that."

When Lydia began to follow their conversation, she recognized two or three childhood friends of Charlie's sitting to the left of the aisle.

She recognized business associates of Tamara Olin's sitting to the right.

Charlie's great aunt sat folding a lace handkerchief over one knee, happily occupying space to the left of the aisle.

Tommy Ballard and his mother had been seated to the right.

Addy Michaels and her grandson had been seated to the left.

Barbara Krug, Tom Olin's Place-Perfect Real Estate secretary, spritzed cologne lightly on both wrists, sending up a cloud of *Emeraude* from the right.

Lydia's whole self began trembling with anger. Even before Charlie and Shelby had arrived, people must have started sitting beside people they agreed with. People were sitting on separate *sides*.

Lydia had her hands on the back of the pew to rise, pressing herself up off of the seat to go she-didn't-know-where.

Maybe just to stand in the middle. Maybe just to stand right smack dab in the center of the aisle.

Her anger and her sense of injustice propelled her to stand. *Just walk away, Lydia. Keep your head down. Just step sideways past everybody's knees and don't tread on anybody's feet.*

She stumbled over Tamara's purse and felt Tom catch her elbow to steady her.

"Miss P," Shelby whispered. "What is it? What's wrong?"

"I'm sorry, Shelby," she whispered back. "I just have to get out of this place."

By this time, Joe Douglas had stepped away from the pulpit and stood at the altar with loving, outstretched arms, his sleeves billowing out like the wings of a crow. The choir members, with upraised chests and pursed mouths, were humming "Just As I Am." One-hundred-and-twenty-some-odd heads were already ducking and peeking to see if someone might be accepting Jesus Christ as Lord, opening a place for Him in their hearts. The music director had already taken them through the a cappella hymn three times.

All those people looking, waiting, expecting someone to stand and walk forward to accept.

Lydia had done that a long time ago. When she'd been a little girl. When she'd thought He'd be big enough to make things work out the way they were supposed to. When she'd thought that to believe in Him dying on the cross meant happy endings. Fairy tales.

When Lydia reached the aisle, she didn't start toward the pulpit, as many people had expected, or stand in the middle of the sanctuary which, in her anger, she had thought she might do.

This is all we are, Lord. We're people; we walk around screwing things up.

With Charlie Stains and Shelby Tatum and Uncle Cy and everybody else in Shadrach wondering what she was doing, Lydia turned and left through the front door.

CHAPTER SIXTEEN

───── ❧ ─────

*T*wo dusty blue Caprice Classics with the Shadrach city crest on their sides drove up to Charlie Stains's small house Monday morning, and parked. Blue flashers turned lethargically, the color bending across lower tree limbs even in the brightest Shadrach sun. Doors opened. Uniformed men unfolded and climbed out. They left their doors open, radios crackling.

Addy Michael, who had been raking maple leaves into a pile in her front yard, paused with the rake handle gripped in both hands. Raymond Ashby, who kept three dried corncobs hanging from a limb to feed the squirrels, picked that moment to step out into his yard and replenish the supply. On the sidewalk where George Nagle and Red Christensen's discussion of the church sermon yesterday had quickly become skewed into a discussion of the fishing weather, both men stopped and stared.

Politely but purposefully, their insignia gleaming, their belts creaking, their shoes making castanet snaps on the pavement, the four officers walked forward and waited for Charlie to answer the door.

"Hello?"

"Would you step outside, please, Mr. Stains?"

Soundlessly, he did so.

"Mr. Charles Frederick Stains," one of the officers recited in a practiced monotone. "Is that you?"

"Yes."

"I have a warrant for your arrest on both felony and misdemeanor counts of alleged criminal sexual misconduct."

They rocked him to one side and secured his hands behind his back.

"You have the right to remain silent. Anything you say can be used against you in a court of law. You have the right at this time to an attorney of your own choosing and to have them present before and during questioning and the making of any statement."

"You're arresting me? Because of Shelby Tatum?"

"If you cannot afford an attorney, you are entitled to have an attorney appointed for you by a court and to have them present before and during questioning and the making of any statement. You have the right to exercise any of the above rights at any time during any questioning and the making of any statement. Do you understand each of these rights I've explained to you?"

Dumbfounded, Charlie nodded.

As neighbors watched from their lawns and curtains were lifted or pulled aside in just about every front window on the street, one of the officers took him by the elbow and led him down the walk. Another officer opened the rear cruiser door, the one with no handle inside.

The city crest on the side of the door said, "The Welfare of the People Shall Be The Supreme Law."

"Get in the car. Please, Mr. Stains."

After he climbed in, the neighbors craned their necks to see him through the metal grate in the squad car. The Caprice pivoted, slewing dust in every direction. The two heads inside passed by in a flash. They caught only a glimpse of the officer with his cap cocked low over his eyes. But behind him they saw a stranger's face, Charlie's mouth set in a grim line, his eyes riveted to the rearview mirror.

❦

LYDIA HEARD THE NEWS after third period on Monday.

During the morning break, she had conducted a meeting with Whitney Allen concerning the girl's behavior at the dance Saturday night. She and L.R. had decided, if Shelby was willing, that they would bring in one of their honor students, a volunteer peer mediator, to oversee the differences between the two girls.

L.R. had been busy for hours in Mayhem Central, fending off the press. The police had been at the school early, asking questions. Now that an arrest had been made, the school was getting calls from as far away as California and Texas.

Missouri live-TV units were parked in the school-bus turnaround, vans with pole-like broadcast antennas cranked toward the heavens.

Rumors abounded that Shelby had arrived at school only to call her mother on the cell phone to take her home.

Nibarger had hired Larry Mortenson, a regular St. Clair County substitute teacher, to take over teaching Charlie's class long term. But, although Larry had reported ready to teach a lesson on parquetry flooring, the police had asked that they be given access to Charlie's classroom before students gathered there. So Lydia invited Charlie's wood-working students to meet in a library study room, where she opened a discussion for the kids to talk.

"You heard he got arrested, didn't you?" Adam announced.

"Yeah," somebody else chimed in. "My mom saw everything out the front window."

"Hey, man," Johnny insisted. "Stains taught me how to design the sideboards for my truck. This reeks."

If anyone had noticed Lydia at that moment, they would only have noticed a slight clench of her jaw, a lowering of her brows. She willed herself not to let them see her react.

"Somebody busted into Shelby's locker. Did you hear that?"

"No way."

"That's why Shelby left this morning. Her parents decided to go ahead and press charges. She got here and all of her stuff was gone."

The bell rang. The kids shoved their chairs back and gathered their notebooks.

Believe me, beloved.

As the children left, nobody noticed that Lydia sat down hard in her chair. She stared at the surrounding bookshelves without seeing them.

"Oh Father," she said aloud.

I'm so tired of hearing all these many voices.

Everybody wants to tell me what they know.

Nobody knows anything.

Only Charlie knows, the thought came. *Only Shelby knows.*

She stood to leave the library. Cassie Meade popped up from behind the 759.4 Dewey Decimal shelf, which contained rows and rows of lavish art books, where she had been hiding.

Cassie clutched a book titled *Picasso, The Art and Times of A Young Painter* against her as she stepped forward.

"I want to show you something," Cassie whispered. "Can I?"

"What?"

"It's something about Mr. Stains," she said. And Lydia's blood froze in her veins. *Not this. Not another girl telling me something else awful about Charlie.*

Fear filled her throat. "What?"

"This." From the pages of the book, Cassie drew a small

pastel drawing signed only with her initials. C. M. The picture was a miniature, only three inches square, an oak tree in winter clinging to its leaves, sketched in tones of brown and gray, its limbs silhouetted like two lifted hands with outspread fingers.

"I wanted to tell you that he couldn't have done it, Miss P. I know."

Lydia fought the urge to grab Cassie's shoulders and shout at her. *How? How do you know?*

"I know it in my heart," Cassie said simply, and Lydia's own heart, which had jumped so very high at that, now sank low. But Cassie was pulling another sheet of paper out of the book. "I know it in my heart because of what he wrote."

"What's this?"

"Judges' comments from the art contest last spring. "And she pointed. "There. Right there. Look what he wrote."

Yes, Lydia recognized the handwriting. The same scrawled, dark shapes that she had seen scribbled on Shelby's homework last week, the same slanting bold print he had used to write notes to her and slip them inside her staff box.

"Go ahead. Read it," Cassie said. And so, Lydia did.

Dear Miss Meade,
I am not an expert on art but, when they asked me if I wanted to add some comment here, I jumped at the chance. This picture reminds me of something I've read that I love,

a verse in the Bible about trees growing with their roots deep in the water. Most people don't know that oak trees do not lose their leaves in winter. You have done a lovely job here of showing both the season and the strength. I feel your picture. And that is the truest form of art that there can be.

Don't ever let yourself shy away from your dream. Always remember that you are put here on this earth to do one certain thing. I guess all of us struggle a long time to find out what that one thing is. You are unique. There is not anyone else waiting in the wings to accomplish the job that you have been set out to do. The future that you wait for is yearning for you to find it. You are a wonderful artist.

Congratulations,
Charlie Stains

"See," Cassie said. "Nobody could write anything like that and do what Shelby says he did."

Lydia read the words again. Charlie's own words. *There is not anyone else waiting in the wings to accomplish the job that you have been set out to do.*

Lydia felt her eyes filling with tears. *What would that be for me, Father? What have I been set out for? If only I could believe that I was that important to You . . . that You had a plan like that for me . . .*

"Will you tell me what I should do?" Cassie asked. "I can't just stand around and let something like this happen to him."

There is such a difference, beloved, between believing and knowing.

After all the times Lydia had asked herself the same question. After all the times she had struggled to figure out which way she should turn.

But that's just it, Lord, don't You see? I've believed in You all my life. But it doesn't feel like anything new anymore. It feels bland and old and irrelevant.

All this time, and she felt like she was reaching past it, around it, beyond it, like the sunglasses she hadn't been able to find on top of her own head.

I thought there were so many things You wanted to give me . . .

Lydia spoke the words by rote, not because she believed them, but because she knew that they were the only ones she could say to Cassie at this moment. "It's just like Mr. Stains wrote. The life you are called to is waiting for you. Some things cannot be changed, no matter what. Maybe it's what you *do* with the unchangeable things that matters."

⬥

"DID YOU HEAR?" Brad asked her when Lydia returned to her cubicle and found him waiting. "They've arrested him."

Even one hour ago, she had tried to cover for herself. She had not let any of the students see her emotion. But Lydia just gazed up at Brad now, her face awash in misery, her heart vulnerable and open, for him to see.

"Did they fingerprint her locker?"

He nodded. "The thing had at least thirty distinct sets of prints on it, including most of Shelby's friends and family. And if Charlie used a key, they're saying he never had to touch the locker at all."

"It wasn't broken into?"

"No," Brad said. "That's the whole significant thing. It was either a teacher with a key or somebody who knew the combination. And it had to be somebody who knew which locker belonged to Shelby."

Lydia stared at the jar of candy Kisses on her desk. She reached for the lid to offer Brad one, anything to break the silence and the aching between them. But the lid slipped out of her hand. It shattered on the desk top. They both jumped at once, stared at it for three or four helpless seconds before reaching for something to sweep up the glass. Then they both stopped.

He said, "I saw you talking to him at Big Tree Baptist yesterday. A person would have to be blind not to see what you feel for him."

She gave up, just stared down at the broken splinters in front of her.

"A person would have to be blind not to see what I see in your face now."

She bit her lower lip, looked up at him.

"There's something between the two of you, isn't there? Or, at least, there *was*."

Lydia didn't speak.

"Which explains why you'd come out to walk on the dock that late alone."

She didn't deny that, either.

"Are you going to tell me anything?" he asked.

She shook her head. *No.*

"Look." He rose from the edge of the table where he'd been leaning. "I came by to thank you for helping get Taylor into the truck the other night. He didn't wake up until morning. He wanted to know if we'd caught any fish."

"What did you tell him?"

"I had to tell him we'd gotten skunked."

"Poor thing." A sad little grin.

"I was going to ask if you wanted to go night fishing with us again. But, I guess, *no*."

"Brad."

He poked his hand inside the open jar and took a fistful of candy. "I'm going to get answers for you, Lydia. I'm going to get answers about Charlie. About his past. I can do that much."

"You don't have to—"

He held up a hand to stop her. "You have to learn to let people do this. Did it ever occur to you that you ought not to feel guilty for what people want to *give* you?"

"But there isn't any reason for you to do anything for

me." She rubbed the ball of her thumb over the bridge of her nose. "There isn't any reason for me to *take* from you."

"This isn't taking." She thought he was reaching for the jar again but he didn't. He wrapped his big hand around her wrist instead, just to reassure her, just to touch her, something that only Charlie would have done. "It's receiving. There's a difference. If I want to, just let me help you."

"But, I don't—"

"What?" he asked when she hesitated. "Don't what?"

"I don't know."

"What were you going to say?"

"It doesn't matter."

"Yes, it does."

"Brad."

"You don't think you deserve it? Is that it?"

She shook her head.

Still, he didn't let her go. "Lydia, I want you to tell me what you were about to say."

She didn't pull away from his grasp. She waited, searching. And when she realized the truth, she felt a scalding heat rush into her lungs. "Maybe. Maybe I was going to say that. Yes, maybe that was it exactly."

For a long moment, they faced off against each other. Finally, he asked it. "Do you think that you don't deserve something when you think that other people *do?*"

She whispered. "Yes."

"Why is that, Lydia? Why do you feel that way? Do you know?"

She had begun to cry in front of Brad, and she hated herself for it. She backhanded her nose.

"Look," he said. "I'm going to prove you wrong. I've got sources at the University of Missouri that I trust. Sources that other people don't have."

"Nibarger couldn't get anything from the university when they called him back this morning. They told him that their past employment records are sealed."

"Maybe I can get something opened," Brad said. "With your permission, I'd like to try."

CHAPTER SEVENTEEN

———— ❦ ————

he two-year-old girl disappeared from the Humbert's Finger Campground sometime after three on Monday afternoon. Lydia heard the police sirens as she dismissed a meeting of volunteers who would be helping her administer an SAT Preparation Workshop next month.

Lydia stood gazing out the window, examining the thing she had discovered about herself—*What is it? What is it that Brad's questions found in me, such a surprise that it made me cry?*—when the chilling chromatic scale of the sirens began.

Her first thought was of Charlie. But, *no,* it couldn't be anything to do with him. Not after he'd been taken into jail this morning. Lydia watched the cruiser lights flickering through the trees even in bright daylight, disappearing toward the outskirts of town.

When the young woman arrived at the school somewhat later to find her, Lydia didn't know what to make of her. The young mother was shivering from shock, draped in a pale yellow quilt. "My husband wouldn't come with me," she said. "He's still down at the campsite, searching through the brush. But I thought I would at least try."

"Try what?" Lydia's blood ran cold, because she already thought she knew, and it was impossible.

"I was reading a book in the tent and I fell asleep. I woke up and she was gone. She wandered away."

"I'm so sorry." Lydia gripped the door jamb. "I'm sure the police are doing everything that they can."

"The newspaper reporter told me about you. His name was—"

"Brad? Brad Gritton?"

"No. Someone else. A Mr. Parker?"

"Oh, yes."

"He was down there, and he said everybody knew your story. He thought that maybe you'd help."

"I don't think I can. I'm sorry."

"We're camped so close to the lake. No one knows whether to look for her on the hill or to look for her in the water. So they're doing both."

"I—I don't know what to tell you. I-I'll pray for you to find your child."

"No." And the woman gripped her arm and wouldn't let her go. "I want you to do more than that."

"There isn't any more than that—"

"The newspaper reporter said that, when you were young, you once found a boy in the forest."

"A lot has happened to me since I was young."

"Come with me, please."

∽

LYDIA MADE NO complaint about how fast the woman was driving, but when the panel van skidded around a corner, Lydia put her shoulder harness on. *I can't do this. I can't do any of this.* And it occurred to Lydia that her life had always been one long journey, longing for something that had once seemed possible, knowing that she faced a total powerlessness now.

"Jamie's wearing a pair of red toddler pants . . . a little shirt with a bluebird on it. Her hair was in a ponytail, but it might have come down. You never know what has happened to it between then and now."

Cars blocked the entrance to the shore at Humbert's Finger. Lydia's ankles twisted on the rocks as they left the van and stumbled down to the campground. What must have once been a peaceful picnic site was now littered with radio equipment and muddy footprints. "I'd say we've got a good two hours of daylight left for a search and rescue," Judd Ogle was announcing, his hands shoved forlornly into the pockets of his pants.

The dogs had already gone out; Lydia could hear them baying to the west. When she appeared, they stared at her. "What are you doing out here?"

The woman stepped out in front of her. "I went to get her. I want her to try and find Jamie."

Lydia said it so softly that not any of them could hear her. "I don't think I can."

"No sense hanging all your hopes on that," another officer said over her. "That's just some Shadrach legend. Things like that don't happen around this place anymore."

"Please," the lady whispered to Lydia. "Don't listen to them."

As Lydia stepped toward an opening in the trees, the woman started to follow her. So did several other people who, for all their arguing against what she could do, seemed oddly interested in the direction she wanted to go. All she really wanted to do was hurry away from them.

She stopped. "I have to go by myself if I'm going to do this."

"We've all read that article in the paper, Miss Porter. You had your father with you before."

She ignored them, thinking only how impossible this was, and was gone. The trees closed in around her like a tunnel, the leathery curls of leaves unfurling beneath her feet. And with each step she took, it seemed like she stepped further and further toward something she didn't understand, further toward something that she wondered if she could trust. *Oh Father Oh Father Oh Father.*

The sounds of the dogs faded further to her left. The hawthorn and the jack oak brambles began to tug like an anxious child at her feet.

All these things people expect of me. I'm so tired of disappointing everybody.

She walked without knowing where she was going. She walked without hearing a word. At last, out of breath, she stopped and hung her head, supporting herself against a shagbark trunk. *Oh, Lord. I'm so tired of trying to find You.*

For a moment, she glanced behind her, thinking she should give up and go back. She wanted to run back to everyone and say, *no no no,* but just then she caught a faint scent of something sweet, oranges, tangy and fresh, like springtime instead of fall. When she turned toward the depths of the trees, a shadow flitted through them.

"Hello?" Of course, she thought, it could have been a bird. "Hey?" She tried to think of the child's name. "Are you here?" Then she remembered it. "Jamie?" Perhaps she should have brought the little girl's mother with her. Anyone that young could be afraid, hearing a stranger calling her name.

You're looking past me, Lydia. Did you know that?

"Jamie? Can you hear me?"

Nothing.

Then Lydia heard the breeze behind her before she felt it, watched it tumble toward her through the crowns of the sycamores. Leaves dislodged and began to sift down around her shoulders. And, as she stepped through them, it seemed as if they almost had a voice.

How I delight in your pursuit of me. But you're looking at me the human way, Lyddie, as if you have to convince me to care, as if you have to struggle to make me hear you.

She moved on, climbing over a rotten stump, coming into a clearing. "Which direction?" She didn't even realize she was asking it out loud. "Which one?"

I chose you before the foundation of the earth. I planned great and marvelous works for you to do. My son died so that I might hear your beloved whisper, that you might follow me along every trail, that you might go where I am.

It was such an odd feeling, this sensation that she must be following something, only she didn't know what it could be. A child wouldn't move this quickly.

To her right came the familiar lapping sounds of water but, as she peered through the limbs, she saw only sky. She had left the Brownbranch, the steel, cold mirror, a long way below. It amazed her how such a gentle rippling sound could carry this far uphill.

Lydia went another way, hedging toward the north, ducking her head so as not to bump it on low-lying branches. Here she found a high ridge where the ground leveled off. The undergrowth opened a little; it wasn't as thick here. "Jamie?"

She should have brought a radio or something. She'd been crazy to run off so fast and not figure out a way to communicate with them. Crazy. They'd probably already found the child, Jamie, or whatever-her-name-was anyway; everybody down there was probably celebrating and laughing, because Lydia Porter was still thrashing around up there, and she had no way to know.

Why should she be heading up a rise like this, looking for a child that could barely walk?

What sort of mother would bring a child camping, and leave it alone while she took a nap?

What sort of heavenly Father would leave anyone lost when they needed the most to find Him?

Oh Father . . .

It wasn't any use. She couldn't do this.

She sat down on a rock and waited. And waited. Waited more. Her bottom grew sore, as the sun ducked behind a western hill.

That you might follow me . . . That you might go where I am . . .

Lydia stood, dusted off the seat of her pants. Unwilling to stop trying, she made broader and broader circles, calling, waiting, searching, listening. But nothing. She'd try a different place. No sense being up here anymore. She started back down and, as she did, she began to hear the lake again, and the dogs, and the sounds of people calling for a child. *Another sad story,* she thought. *Another broken, awful, unexplainable thing happening in the world.*

That's when her foot kicked something hidden beneath the leaves. She bent to pick it up. It was a toddler's toy, a plastic face with a sleeping cap and lime-green segments, the thing that helped a child when it was afraid of the dark. A Glo-Worm.

She squeezed the toy's body and the face lit brightly in the waning forest light. It hadn't been here long enough to even get soiled. The battery still burned fresh.

Lydia held the thing up and questioned the merry eyes, the broad, silly grin. "What's happened here, you," she demanded of Glo-Worm. "Because I know you could tell me." She swung in a broad circle, looking again. She had just decided to cry out the girl's name when something stopped her.

Clarity. Peace. Her instincts did not just suggest she do this thing; they demanded it. Lydia surveyed the trees around her, chose a stout, loose-limbed hickory. She tied her Nikes tighter and began to climb.

After she reached a good height she did not have to search long. There, five paces off to her left, she glimpsed a flash of small, red pants. Jamie had curled herself up in the rootwell of a sycamore.

For one brief, spellbinding moment, Lydia was terrified that the child had fallen or gotten injured. But she held her own breath for three beats, four, and listened.

Yes, sound does travel uphill.

Lydia heard the melodic rhythm of a baby's peaceful breathing, resting in sleep, unafraid.

~

THERE WOULD BE, of course, another story in the newspaper.

It had been close to 6:00 p.m. when she awakened the little girl and kept her smiling all the way to the campground with the Glo-Worm. After that, all Lydia had wanted to do was get home.

Now she folded open the lid to the mailbox the way she did every night when she arrived, the way she did on any ordinary evening, although this day did not feel like anything ordinary at all.

She sifted through the bills and the flyers, separating the personal envelopes from junk mail and bank statements. And, so odd. Along with everything else, today seemed to be a day of letters. She found, when she thumbed through the envelopes, that she'd gotten two of them.

Lichen Bridge, CT
October 6

Our Dearest Lydia,
Haven't heard from you in so long and your dad and I have been wondering what's been going on in your life! Was so glad to get the e-mail about you buying your plane tickets and everything being set for Christmas. You should see Dad, already being excited about that. It isn't even Thanksgiving yet, and he comes in yesterday with a clock he bought at Wal-Mart that plays Christmas carols every hour. Like those birds that chirp every hour, only this one plays songs. $24.99 for that thing, when he wouldn't buy a fishing license from Cy last time because the out-of-state day fee was too much. I get to hear "Joy to the World" every day at three in the after-

noon, and at three in the morning, although it has a sensor on it and, when there isn't any light, it plays much softer. Maybe it will run out of batteries?!

So now you know how your father feels about you coming home. ☺

Wanted to write and let you know about an odd thing that happened the other day. A woman came to our door and said she knows you. Or that she knows of you, and she'd like to be in touch. I gave her your address before your father said it might not be the right thing to do. I hope I wasn't wrong?! Anyway, you may hear from her soon. She said she'd be 'A Blast From Your Past.' I think it's got something to do with homecoming at your own high school. Maybe she's somebody you knew there? If it's a problem I gave her your address, then it's my fault.

Until soon. I'm going to a class to learn how to e-mail. Right now, though, it's faster to just write by hand.

Anything interesting happening with your students? You are a wonderful girl, sweetheart, and I know you are helping everybody you meet. We have always been so proud of you.

We are both excited and intrigued about getting to meet your 'friend.' I think that's why your father bought that clock, too. He's wondering if you might be bringing home a man?! (Although how Christmas carols in the night would help with that situation, I don't know.) You know I would never write and ask you these things! Marla Tompkins did stop me the other day at Pendergrass to see if I had any grandchildren?! Of course she had pictures of hers. Why do people ask these nosy questions? One of her grandchildren has very big ears but, you will be proud, I did not say a word about that, either.

> *With so much love,*
> *Mother*

Lydia couldn't help it. Her heart went heavy again.

Things are so different than I had thought they would be. I had so many of my own plans.

She opened the second letter.

Lichen Bridge, CT
October 7

Dear Miss Porter:

This may seem like an odd letter to you but I feel it is something I ought to do. I stopped by your parents' house the other day and your mother gave me your address. I hope you don't mind my getting in touch.

My ex-husband, Clive Buckholtz, passed away several months ago and I have been asked to sort through his personal affects for the family. I don't know if you will remember Clive or not. He was known as Mr. Buckholtz and taught Junior English at your school in Lichen Bridge. In with some of his more important papers and household ledgers, he kept an envelope with your name on it.

I hope you don't mind that I opened the envelope and looked inside. The only thing in the envelope was a test from his class. It is an essay exam with in-depth questions about Beowulf. *On this test you scored a moderate grade, a mid-B.*

He left a note on top of the envelope that, should anything ever happen to him, I was to find you and make sure you had this paper. Even his note, I'm afraid, was written a long time ago. I haven't seen Clive in years. He had not taught in the public schools since his retirement in 1991. I am staying at a rental cottage while in Lichen Bridge to finish sorting through these things. Unfortunately, I do not have a phone. The rental office has one, but that is three miles up the road! If this old test holds any significance to you, you may contact me at the return address below and I will send it to you posthaste. I did not want to mail it out unless I was certain I had the correct Miss Lydia Porter. But, since I've talked to your mother, I do think it's you.

> *Respectfully,*
> *Jolena Criggin (Formerly Buckholtz)*
> *234 Plumb Hill Road*
> *Straddle Ridge Rental Cottages*

Lydia laid this in her lap without refolding it. She stared at it a long time. She realized that she needed to breathe.

. . . like a tree planted by the water . . .

It's what we do with the unchangeable things that matters. Isn't that exactly what she'd said to Cassie Meade?

Beloved, don't you see where I've been leading you?

Well.

Well.

Lydia folded the letter and placed it back inside its envelope. She dialed the Olins' telephone number. Once connected, she asked Tamara for permission to invite Shelby to travel along with her.

Oh, Lord. If You'd show me the difference between believing and knowing.

With all the help that she'd offered Shelby, maybe she hadn't yet offered anything of her heart at all.

If You're close to me, God.

If this is what You want from me . . .

The heavenly Father had just gotten more unpredictable than ever.

♾

WEEKLY VISITATION at the St. Clair County Jail began at seven Monday night. It lasted for two hours. Lydia had struggled across the parking lot at Winn-Dixie, trying to make it there on time, with the wind so strong it had blown all the loose shopping carts backward. Once she made it to Osceola, she pulled in to the jail lot off Chestnut Street, the Buick headlights catching pinstripes of rain, and parked in the designated visitor space. She covered her head with the only thing available in her front seat, a college admittance application from Bowling Green, and climbed out.

A cool rain had been drizzling all afternoon again, the typical weather pattern for autumn. The grounds back at the high school looked more like a pig-wrestling arena than a place to play soccer.

Lydia tried to yank open the jail door, but it wouldn't budge. A second or two ticked by before she realized she needed to press a bell and signal her presence. Behind a window inside, a uniformed lieutenant glanced up, checked her out.

She must have passed inspection. The door buzzed and a latch clicked open. It unnerved her when she stepped inside the crowded waiting room.

The guard waited for her behind a glass partition that must have been at least five inches thick. "It clearing up out there?" he asked, as if visiting somebody in the lockup was something you did every day.

"Clear up to our eyeballs." Of course, she had to say that. She was used to bantering with teenagers.

He shoved a clipboard through a small furrow. A pencil dangled from the clipboard with a length of soiled, ancient string. "Need to fill this out. Your name. His name. Time signed in. Relationship to inmate."

Lydia Porter, she scribbled. *Charlie Stains. 7:46 p.m.* Friend.

"Thanks," he said, looking it over. "It'll be twenty minutes or so. There's not room for him at the window right now. Take any seat."

"Thank you."

"I mean, don't *take* it. They might lock you up for stealing. Wouldn't want to spend any time in the slammer. Ha ha ha."

In the end, Lydia waited much longer than twenty minutes. She waited while a mother with young children went in, then a squatty man who talked with his hands. She stopped thinking of it as waiting after a while. Seeing Charlie like this wasn't the sort of thing she knew how to wait for. She was just *there*, taking the next punch anybody wanted to throw at her. When at last the warden stepped out and gestured for her, it almost felt like a surprise.

"You got fifteen minutes in there, Miss Porter. They're bringing him in."

Inside a cubicle that wasn't much larger than a closet, three chairs sat like stools facing a soda fountain. With two of them already taken, visitors sat elbow to elbow. Lydia wedged her way in beside them, scooting the third seat forward like she was scooting up to the supper table.

Through this glass panel, she faced an empty chair.

Charlie rounded the corner with wardens at his elbows and wrists wrapped in chains. He saw her and his entire body went rigid. A hollow knot appeared at the juncture of his jaw.

She couldn't help flinching when she saw him. The outfit was dreadful. An orange jumpsuit with St. Clair County Jail emblazoned over his left pectoral.

No buttons, only snaps. And short sleeves. Charlie never wore short sleeves. Sleeveless, maybe, or torn-away T-shirts when he worked on the dock in the sun. But never anything like this.

She focused on the jumpsuit to keep from focusing on his face.

The wardens unlocked his handcuffs and stood guard over him. He folded doggedly into the chair. Two phones hung on the wall between them, one on his side, one on hers. She picked up the receiver. He didn't.

They stared at each other for a good four minutes. When he finally got on line with her, there they sat. She listened to him breathe. Even *that* sounded tinny and unreal, as if Charlie was breathing somewhere on the other side of the earth.

"You're getting out tomorrow?" she whispered.

No answer.

"If they determine probable cause tomorrow, then they'll set bail?"

His eyes, his breathing, pinned her. She felt herself teetering but gritted her teeth, forced her eyes to stay dry, her voice to stay steady.

"Is there anything you need me to—?"

He jumped on that with copperhead speed. "There was only one thing I needed from you." With his arm pressed against the counter, his elbow bearing all his weight. "I needed you to believe me."

And then, the breathing again.

Outside in the waiting room, a toddler shrieked. A chair scuffed the floor when the warden announced "Time's up" for someone else down the row. Rain drummed on the roof, a distant, mysterious sound. More melancholy and miraculous, that sound, because some people in this place hadn't seen rain for a very long time.

As minutes lumbered past, he sat with his forehead braced in his palm. She thought she should say something, but helplessness kept her still. When he moved at last, he lifted his entire face through the grip of his fingers. "Look, Lydia," he said as he stretched out his chin. And something subtle had changed in his voice. "This is more difficult than I thought it would be."

"Yes." It was all she could say.

Ridiculous, after all that waiting and breathing, that each of them jumped in with something at the same moment to say.

"I told them I would—" Charlie muttered.

"I came to tell you—" Lydia rushed.

"I hired Tuck Herrington as a lawyer."

"I think you should know that I'm going away."

Lydia waited for his response to that, to her going away.

So much in her heart right now that she couldn't explain.

Using this odd letter to put distance between herself and Shadrach, to put distance between herself and Charlie.

Running toward something that she could never escape. And taking Shelby with her.

At the St. Clair County Jail, the second hand on the industrial clock moved with terse, short jerks.

"Harrington and I were in Scouts together. I told him I would take a lie-detector test. But he won't let me do it."

"I'm leaving early in the morning, Charlie. I wanted you to know that's why I won't be in the courtroom when they set your bail and give you the arraignment date. If I was going to be here, I would be at the courthouse."

She stopped rambling and stared at him as if she'd just heard him for the first time. "I don't understand." And her heart dared to surge. *A lie-detector test? How simple was that?*

"Lie-detector results aren't admissible in court. But if I take it and something goes wrong and I don't pass, Harrington thinks it'll give the prosecutors more to work with." It had taken him this long to hear her, too. "Where are you going?"

"Home." Hard to explain. Nobody had ever known anything about this. "There's something in Lichen Bridge that I have to resolve."

She waited for Charlie's boiling questions, his accusations. Those didn't come.

"I don't know how long I'll be gone. Maybe a week."

"I'm sorry, Miss Porter. Your visiting time is over."

Lydia jerked her face toward the clock. The wardens had appeared out of nowhere. They were standing over Charlie, waiting with keys and chains. Another guard appeared at her side to usher her out.

"No, *wait*."

"I'm sorry, Miss Porter. You knew from the beginning how much time you had."

No seconds wasted as they stood him up sideways. His ear was still cocked to the phone.

"Listen to me," he said quietly. "Just listen to me." The first thing he'd said for fifteen minutes that carried any urgency, as if this one statement he wanted to make carried the weight of the world for him.

"You have to give us time to talk about one more thing," she begged the guard while, with a frightening economy of motion, the warden secured Charlie's wrists in cuffs. "Please give us just a little more time."

"I give you more time, lady, I have to give it to everybody."

"I'm leaving town tomorrow," she pleaded. "He's telling me about a lie-detector test."

"Honey, you don't understand. Everybody in this place has important things to talk about. You don't just take a turn at the window and talk about the mashed potatoes or the weather. You've got to make it *count*."

"Please."

A deep sigh from the guard, shaking his head, a signal with raised fingers to the others through the glass. "One more minute," he said. "Just one more minute." Then shook his head and shrugged as if to say, *We've got another one of* those.

The wardens pivoted Charlie back toward her, each of them taking one step aside. This had to be it. No words wasted. There wasn't time.

"That lie-detector test . . ." He bit his lips. His nose

turned red. His brows narrowed, a man staring into the face of a storm.

"What?"

He cleared his throat and started over.

"I couldn't understand why you couldn't just stand beside me and shake your fist at the world with me and say, 'Yes Charlie, I believe you.' I couldn't understand why you couldn't say, 'I believe *in* you.' I wanted to risk that stupid lie-detector test for *you*, Lydia. Forget the courts. Forget what Tuck or anybody else said. Forget if it would hurt my case in the long run and send me off to the Missouri Pen. I wanted to do it because the only thing that mattered to me was what you were thinking about me."

A numbing surge of adrenaline rushed through her head, her ears. She held up her left hand, palm out. *Stop.*

"If I've asked too much of you, Lydia, just take it as a rough compliment." Staring hard at her outstretched hand. "Take it as a compliment that I thought you'd be able to give me that much. The next time I see you—"

The wardens moved in on him.

"Minute's up, Mr. Stains. We'll escort you to your cell."

They tried to wrestle the receiver away from him. For this one more sentence, he lodged the receiver down under his chin and wouldn't let go.

"I want you to bring my ring back. I can't make choices because of you anymore, Lydia."

"Charlie."

"It's the wrong thing for you. It's the wrong thing for me. Let's just—"

"I don't want you to make choices for me. I never asked you to—"

The wardens wrenched the phone away from him mid-sentence. They linked their arms through his elbows, jerking him away.

The chair stood empty and desolate on the other side of the glass.

The dead phone hung heavy in her hand.

No matter the astonishing day, the way the missing little girl had been found above the Brownbranch. Watching Charlie's shoulders roll forward away from her, carrying the weight of the chained cuffs, she felt as if she were the one who had just been slammed in jail.

CHAPTER EIGHTEEN

By the time the rain had stopped again sometime just after daybreak, Lydia and Shelby had already driven past the lake. This stretch of road between Warsaw and Sedalia didn't have much scenery. Just a distant mirage of harvest-land dipping like a calm sea, the road edged by an old stake-and-rider fence, a pleasing smattering of trees, a small yellow arrow pointing east that read YOU HAVE JUST MISSED THE TURN-OFF TO KNOB NOSTER.

Shelby had fallen asleep with her mouth hanging open, her head tilted against the headrest at an angle that made Lydia's neck ache. In the air from the open window, feathery tendrils of the girl's blonde hair lifted like living things, whirling around her pale cheeks.

Lydia's silent tears had dried in the soft morning, in the cool strong rush of dry wind. As the miles coursed past beneath the tires, her thoughts rocketed between Jolena

Criggin's letter—*in-depth questions about Beowulf . . . if this holds any significance to you . . .* Buckholtz's class . . . Advance Placement English—to Charlie.

As a Kansas City radio station played *Sweet Home, Alabama,* a great song that wouldn't die, she stared out through the windshield and thought, *He's gone, isn't he, Lord? And all because You finally let him see what I couldn't be.*

When they hit the Interstate and turned east on I-70 toward St. Louis, she realized that something had shifted inside of her about Charlie. Not the human nature shift, where the one who decides to break something finds himself broken instead. No, this was something else entirely. Like a weathervane oiled and gently left turning, she felt like she was wavering into the wind.

As St. Louis towered over their heads with its miles of skyscrapers and fashion billboards and roads dispersing in every direction like tangled cables, Shelby moaned and lifted her head. She smacked her lips and swallowed, stared out through the windshield with narrowed eyes. "Where are we?"

"Guess."

"I don't know."

Thousands of trucks and cars shot past them, racing at what seemed like ridiculous speeds. "Ah!" Shelby jumped, twisting toward the steering wheel even though she was belted in. An SUV merged halfway into their lane and then swerved back when Lydia wouldn't move over.

"How long have I been asleep?"

"A long time."

"This isn't St. Louis. It can't be St. Louis already."

"Time flies when you're sound asleep." Lydia rolled the window down again to greet the acrid rubber and carbon smells of heavy traffic. "Ah, the smell of the city." She felt they needed it—the pleasure of the music cranked up, their hair tugging in the wind, strands tossed by the air in front of their faces.

Shelby pivoted sideways in the seat again and tried to give Lydia a high-five.

A grin. "You think I can do that while I'm driving in this city traffic, you've got more confidence than I do." Her elbows had unclenched a little bit, but Lydia was still driving with both hands.

"You saved that little girl, Miss P. We have to celebrate."

"We aren't going to celebrate while we're moving sixty-five miles an hour."

"But we've gotten away from Shadrach, Miss P." Shelby picked up a package of wintergreen Lifesavers and sliced a seam in the paper. She lifted the next candy with the flick of one peeling peach fingernail. "Here."

Lydia opened her mouth sideways and Shelby slid it in.

"We're just *us*. You and *me*." Then, like a song. "*Me* and Miss *P*."

An hour later, they had stopped for a snack and were heading into Illinois. With sandwich foil blooming like lilies in their laps, picking lettuce off their legs where it had fluttered free, arguing over who got the one cup holder in the Buick's fold-out armrest, they soared along the open road, searching new territory with no one to stop them. And Lydia did her best to concentrate on Shelby, not on the stunning moments when she remembered that Charlie had been arrested, or that he wanted his ring back, or that she'd found a lost little girl in the woods. She focused on the girl beside her, not on the sorrow that lay behind her. She focused on someone she knew she needed to care for, not on the questions that lay before her. She didn't think about her life tilting. She didn't think about there being nothing stable beneath her feet.

The harvested cornfield to the south of the interstate looked like a child who'd been forced into a bad haircut for the first day of school.

"Did you know—" She talked about nothing around a hunk of hamburger bun, trying to bring herself back for the girl beside her. "—that you should always get your hair cut in the new of the moon?"

Shelby stared out of the window at the cornfield. She took a sip of soda.

"Or else your hair will get stringy. Like that cornfield over there."

"That can't be true."

"It's true. At least that's what they say in Missouri. It's an old Ozark tale."

"Yeah, but we aren't in Missouri anymore."

Lydia smiled toward the windshield. "Things can't be true in one place and not be true in another."

"No?"

"No."

Lydia drove on for miles after that, with Shelby drawing curlicues with fries in the ketchup on a napkin.

"Why *did* you bring me, Miss P?" the girl asked finally.

Lydia's hands playing over the steering wheel as she teased. "Maybe just because I wanted someone to help me unwrap my hamburger while I was driving."

Shelby didn't fall for it. "*No*. I'm really serious. I want to know."

"Do you?"

A nod.

"I felt like I should," Lydia said. "That's it. It made me peaceful, thinking of having you with me. What do you think?"

"I think that sounds nice."

"Really?"

"Yeah."

Lydia grinned, "Did you bring your driver's permit with you? Do you feel sure enough of yourself to spell me?"

"You want me to *drive*?"

"Sure. What do you think?"

"Oh, *yes*." Shelby bonked her head on the roof, she bounced so high.

"Don't hurt yourself." A sideways glance and a little grin. "You sure?"

Another bounce of joy. "*Yes*, I'm sure. I've practiced a lot with Tom."

"Okay. If you think you're ready. It's fine with me."

"I'm *ready!*" She unzipped her purse, scrabbled around in it until she brought out the much-prized scrap of paper. With a vast amount of confidence, she waggled her permit in the air. "Tom told me I was doing really well. He said he thought I'd be okay on a highway if I ever wanted to try." She surveyed the horizon that seemed to curve off of the edge of sky. "When you live in Shadrach, you have to drive a long way to find a wide road."

There wasn't much else that needed to be said.

The city park they found when they exited at Vandalia suited their every purpose. The fast-food trappings, which had seemed to mushroom in the sack on the front seat, were tossed into a rusty metal drum. The swings swayed lazily in the breeze, moving as if some child had just run away from them. A shredded soccer goal, its cords billowing and falling like cobwebs, squatted sideways beside an open patch of grass.

Shelby made a wary circle around the goal. For the first time Lydia realized that, since the dance, she hadn't even talked about replacing her soccer ball. Lydia made a mental note to stop somewhere and get her a new one. A big sporting-goods shop in a city, where they could find something colorful from The World Cup. Or maybe one endorsed by Mia Hamm.

For now, though, it didn't seem to matter. Shelby played

air-soccer, sidestepping, zigzagging nothing between her feet, shooting masterfully for a score.

"Very good!" Lydia applauded.

"Thank you."

For Lydia there were leaves in this place, plenty of maple leaves to wade through. Hundreds of leaves, thousands of leaves, deep enough to pick up armfuls and fling overhead. Then the teeter-totter, which Shelby straddled like a seven-year-old, lifting it with the handle.

"Come do this with me!"

"Oh, good grief. It's been years."

Teeter-tottering does come back. The heavy rivets in the middle, the chain that dangled and locked it down. The handlebars, which seemed much lower and smaller than they ever used to seem. The broad seat that had to be straddled like a fat Shetland pony. Oh, yes, and the splinters. Both of them were screaming, trying not to scoot.

"When I was a little kid," Lydia said as she soared up and Shelby went down, "Uncle Cy used to gather all the leaves from the whole place for my Christmas present. He'd rake for weeks, getting that skirt of land clear beside the marina. He'd bag them up with the idea that, when we all came in for the holidays, he'd burn them." Shelby went up and Lydia went down. "But he'd dump them out the first day we got there and we'd turn cartwheels and hide in them. We pulverized them, running through them. He had to gather driftwood from the lakeshore if he wanted a bonfire."

Up and down they went. Up. Down.

"Once, when I was a little girl?" and Lydia loved the way the girl's voice lilted up at the end of her sentences. "My real dad, not Tom, but my real dad? Before he and my mom split up, he built me a tree house and we spent the night there. It was really fun. After he left, it fell apart, though. My mom wouldn't let me climb in it anymore. It made me really sad."

"You ought to see if your dad would come build it again. When I was little, I got a unicycle for Christmas."

"When I was little I wanted a drum . . ."

". . . and I wanted a monkey . . ."

And on and on they went, until the sky and the earth and the world had gone up and down so many times that they both felt silly and dizzy.

&

SHELBY TOOK FINE to the driving. It had been smart, coming off into town so she could get a feel for the LeSabre on slower roads. She leaned forward with her foot plastered to the brake, shifted *plunk-thump* into drive.

Her first mash of the gas pedal surged them forward.

Lydia fought to keep from saying it aloud. *Okay, Shelb, turn on your blinker and signal. Keep your speed on the entrance ramp, you'll do fine. Don't worry about that truck; ease on out into your lane. There you go.*

After ten minutes of sitting a little too forward in the seat, keeping her forearms a little too stiff, glancing a few times too often over her shoulder toward her blind spot,

Shelby leaned into the seat, relaxed her elbows, and found the rearview mirror again. Lydia offered her a piece of Dentyne. Another half hour and she was still chomping on the same piece of gum, humming to the radio, flipping her hair out of her eyes, as if she'd been driving on an interstate every day of her life.

Then she kept her eyes straight on the dotted center line and started to giggle.

"What are you laughing at?"

"That thing in your yearbook."

"What thing?"

Shelby rolled her eyes. "'I know you will go far in life, especially with the rhino noise.'"

"Oh." Lydia rolled her eyes. "*That*."

Driving along, both of them staring straight ahead and grinning.

"Well?"

"Well, what?"

"You going to do it?"

Lydia left her arms crossed over her thighs and stared at the headliner in the Buick. "Let's see." She was thinking.

"Come on, *please*."

Lydia took a deep breath through her nose that went clear down to her pelvis. Let the breath out. Pursed her lips and shook her head again. "Naw."

"Okay. Never mind. Don't do it. Don't—"

It came from beneath Lydia's throat, her mouth closed

and set in a firm line, a guttural bubbling moan that vibrated the whole car.

"Oh, my *word*."

"Watch your lane."

"Oh, my *word*."

"You're going to get us killed. You're weaving all over the road."

∽

LYDIA TOOK OVER the wheel again late in the night. She drove while Shelby drifted off to sleep. A few headlights pinpointed the darkness; she had no sense of distance, couldn't figure out how far ahead of her they were. Every now and then, an eighteen-wheeler would burst past from behind, barreling along in the fast lane, wheels whining at ear level, yellow watery streams of light that your eyes could still see after they had gone.

When she grew sleepy herself, she pulled off onto the shoulder. The night was endless around her; it felt like the roof had disappeared off the sky.

She leaned her seat back and turned her head sideways, taking one private, long look at the girl.

Shelby slept with her cheekbone propped in one hand, her other hand cupped slightly over the saddle of her hipbone.

Her breath came in silent belly-rises the way the young always breathe. Only once or twice did Lydia hear an audible sigh.

There was nothing to keep Lydia company on this empty

221

stretch of highway, nothing except for the stars. She thought of the first time she had really looked at Shelby's birdlike hands, the fingernails chewed to the nubs. She thought of Sam's proud little chip of a diamond blinking in the sun, a symbol, NO TRESPASSING. She thought of how she'd looked at Shelby's hands that day in her office, had heard the things Shelby was saying, had cried out for Charlie, had thought how those teenager hands could have once been her own hands, too.

A slight breeze, the song of the trees, an intuition speaking within her that, even though she had cried out for it, she had almost forgotten how to hear.

Oh, Father. Show me. Please let me see and know what You want from this.

Maybe they should have spent the night somewhere. Lydia closed her eyes and stretched her neck against the backrest. This was a long drive to be making alone. Or with a teenaged girl, for that matter. When people on one end knew you'd left but people on the other end didn't know you were on the way.

Truth alone will never set anyone free, beloved. But it is in the knowing of the truth that you will be changed.

Lydia started the car, loving the heater for the warm air it chugged on her legs. She glanced again at Shelby and steered out, pressed the accelerator to speed. Six hours on either side of silence. Maybe a person really could hear God. Maybe in all this stillness, if you weren't just trying to grab it the way you grabbed a sandwich at the diner, not taking it on your own terms, in your own time.

Your insides have been a hard and crusty rock, Lydia. Use the sledgehammer of My Word to chisel away your hurt, to understand My love. And you will come to know . . .

"Oh, Lord," she whispered aloud. "Can You hear me? Do You know what I'm asking of You?"

And she drove on until morning thinking she was alone.

CHAPTER NINETEEN

———— ❧ ————

*O*h, my goodness! I can't *believe* this. I absolutely cannot *believe* this." The neighbors must have heard
the squalling sound clear down to Simms Road. "What a
surprise. Isn't this fun, Jim, having her drive up like this? So
much more fun, because it wasn't even *planned*."

"Hey, Lyd." Her father's hard, long arms around her,
taking her in. "You look tired. Everything okay?"

"Yeah, Dad." One of those things you said when you
were just coming in the driveway. Later, if she had a chance
to say that her work had been hard, at least she could tell
him that much. "Everything's fine."

"Good. I like to hear that."

"Mom. Dad. I'd like to introduce you to my—" The
door opened on the far side of the Buick and swung wide.

"Oh, my *goodness*," Nancy hollered again, cradling her

cheeks in her palms. "Oh, I just *knew* it. I just knew something was going on."

"What?"

"I just *knew* you wouldn't be able to wait until—"

Nancy glanced over at the car again and froze. Shelby had gotten out and stood with her fingers touching the chrome.

"I'd like to introduce you to my friend, Shelby Tatum."

"Hello," Shelby said, blushing.

"These are my parents. Jim and Nancy Porter."

"Hello." Nancy tried to pretend she hadn't missed a beat.

Jim stepped forward and made a flourish of shaking the girl's hand. "We're so glad to have you here, young lady. Two beautiful women to grace our supper table in the evening."

Nancy was still trying to figure it. A woman's intuition. She'd been expecting someone else to climb out of the car. No matter what was going on, Nancy always seemed to know. "We just thought—"

"It's okay, Mom." Lydia draped her arm across her mother's shoulders and walked with her inside.

"Oh, Shelby, honey. We are just *very* glad to have you, too."

Lydia sighed when she entered the door. It was nice to walk in and have this house be lived in. Newspapers were tossed on the piano bench. Yard-work shoes were plopped beside the mudroom door, one foot still in front of the other, the way they'd been when they'd left her dad's feet. Open mail fanned in a stack on the kitchen table.

So much more cozy, the way it was now, than the lemon-oiled coffee table and the flowers on the countertop and the clean towels hanging on the racks.

Those things made her feel too much like a guest.

"You got bags, Lyd?" Then, to Shelby, "You got a suitcase, young lady? Let's have those Buick keys. I'll bring everything in."

"That's okay, Mr. Porter. I'll get it."

"Nonsense."

"Here, Dad." A wink at Shelby. "We each have one bag. It might be too much for you. We'd better help."

Of course, when they went outside, he didn't open the trunk. He went straight to the hood and clanged it open instead. "Hm-m-mm. Engine looks good. How's the car running?" The hot engine was still ticking. He checked a hose-fitting or two.

"It's doing great, Dad. That alternator is really hanging in there. It certainly did fine on this trip."

"Belts okay?" He yanked one.

"Yep, think so."

Inside again, Nancy had coffee on, sugar cubes out, and cookies on a plate. The house smelled like pot roast. Lydia had forgotten what it was like to walk into a place with kitchen smells. She was always running out for a deli chicken or pasta-to-go in a paper tent.

She left her bag in a corner beside the bed. She ignored

the stack of clean sheets already waiting from her mom. She would get to those later, and help Shelby with hers, too.

On the way through the house, she checked her father's office, snapped the bathroom light on then off again, made a pass through the living room, which was as usual formal, cool, and dark.

She found Shelby settled at the piano. She was plinking out the first few bars to "Chopsticks" while she examined a row of framed photographs lined up behind the music stand. She nodded toward a picture of cousins when they were very small. "Which one are you?"

"That one. Right there. See. With all the crooked teeth."

"How old were you?"

"Trying to remember. Seven, I guess."

"Who are all these other people?"

"My cousins. That's Laurie. And Amy. Oh, and Bill. Right there. This other picture is Mom and Dad in Hawaii. And there, that's college graduation."

"Cool."

She pointed to the last in the row. "This was Ben, the Border collie. We had him when I first got braces."

"Good old Ben." Her dad sloshed coffee out of his mug as he creaked down into his chair. The Christmas clock suddenly erupted into song. "The First Noel." They'd made it in good time; all that driving and they'd gotten in before five. "You like my clock?" Jim asked.

Mention of the clock brought them back to thoughts

about Christmas, only two months away. Nancy popped in from the kitchen, drying her hands on a tea towel.

"We're glad you're home, honey," she said, looking worried and ringing her hands into a knot. "And it's very nice that you've brought Shelby with you. I didn't mean to react the way I did out there. It's just that—"

Jim took the conversation from her. "It's just about your trip home for Christmas. You've planned *that* so far ahead."

"Here." Lydia sat beside Shelby on the piano bench and encouraged her to move her hands down an octave. "You know 'Heart and Soul'?"

"Yeah."

"If you'll do the bottom part, I'll do the top part."

"Sure." The playing began.

"We were so excited to hear you got reasonably priced tickets, honey," Nancy said. "Especially since you had to buy *two*. You said that, Lydia. You said 'I got *our* tickets.' I wrote you about it, remember? You said you were bringing a friend."

Lydia hit a wrong note.

She stared across at the music stand.

"Did I?"

Oh, Charlie. Charlie. It was meant to be so different from this.

"I'm sorry," she fudged, her blood pounding. "I probably said something I didn't mean."

Nancy hung up the tea towel and dropped herself in the

brown tweed swivel chair. Shelby asked if she could trade and do the top half of "Heart and Soul."

"Sure." Lydia scooted over so Shelby could come around.

"Nancy." Jim lifted his mug to his wife in a toast. He lifted his eyebrows, too. "More coffee? Please?"

"I wanted to hear all about these *plans*, Jim." She took another bite out of the cookie and continued rather insistently, "Lydia, you don't know how overjoyed we are about this. We're planning an open house sometime Christmas week so we can have everybody over. Aunt Ruby and Uncle Arthur will want to stop by. And the Beamans. It will be the perfect time to have the Beamans. I want them all to have a chance to meet your young man."

Lydia's hands slipped on the piano keys. A C-major chord turned into something much less pleasant.

Shelby frowned over at Lydia's wrist.

"Mother. Stop. *Listen*."

Oh, why did I forget this? Why did I forget that it's this way every time I come home?

"I *know* what I heard you say, Lydia. You *said* 'I got *our* tickets.' "

But it was Shelby who asked beneath her breath, touching Lydia's wrist with her left pinkie. "Miss P? *What* young man?"

Lydia laid her right hand over Shelby's left one. To anyone watching her fingers, she was very calm. But everything inside her had turned to rough stone.

"Are you *never* going to get serious about anybody, Lydia?

How old do you have to be before you settle down? Get a husband? Get yourself some babies?"

"Some people decide just not to do that sort of thing."

"Well." Nancy Porter slapped her knees in frustration. "*I've* decided you need to do that sort of thing. And a mother's heart ought to be worth something."

"There is no one, Mama. I'm sorry. I'm not dating anybody. I'm not seeing anybody. I'm not bringing anybody here for the holidays." How bitter these words tasted. Not only because she'd wanted it to be different for her mother, but mostly because she'd wanted it to be different for herself. What she'd felt for Charlie, what she still felt for him, had taken her somewhere deeper than wanting these things. She had wanted to stand beside him. She had wanted to know him while he grew old. She had wanted to nurse him through the flu and punch him when he snored and see his children grow to resemble him more each year. "There's just going to be me."

With a disappointed *humph*, Nancy shoved off with her Naturalizer-clad toe on the carpet. "I was so *sure* that's what you had planned." The chair swiveled until she faced the North Pole instead of the equator. "And Marla Tompkins with enough grandchildren, she'd like to give some away."

CHAPTER TWENTY

*E*very step Lydia made along Plumb Hill Road brought her closer to Jolena Criggin's rental cottage. Every step brought her closer to the moment for which she had driven all these miles. And every step brought her closer to the place where she'd been left alone by a heavenly Father when she'd cried out to Him, long ago, from her purest heart.

This was not anything that could have been swept away with a phone call or put to rest with a scribbled letter.

Not when someone like Mr. Buckholtz had left behind what he'd left behind.

With a false air of nonchalance, Lydia had made a jaunt to the Straddle Ridge rental office and asked the man to point out the way. He'd drawn a squiggly line on a map.

"Nice lady," he'd said when she told him who she was coming to see. "Such a shame about her ex-husband, though. Must be a hard job going through someone's things."

"I imagine it would be."

"Look. She gave me this." He pulled a leather compass case out of his pocket, popped open the steel snap, and showed her the compass inside, the unscratched glass, the vacillating needle. "Used to be his." He shrugged. "Guess nobody wanted it."

When he gave her the map, Lydia folded it into careful, tiny squares, pressing each crease hard twice. "Thank you." And she poked it inside the pocket of her sweater where she could touch its edges and feel that it was still there.

In her car, she unfolded the map and followed it. She parked at the curb, walked the width of three cottages because there was no place closer to leave the car.

I was crazy, wasn't I?

Thinking that fifteen years ago, God heard me. Thinking that any of this could make a difference now.

At that moment, trudging up the narrow fieldstone walk, Lydia came face to face with hope. Hope she hadn't known could still be there.

If God is going to do something, how many years does it take for Him to answer a prayer?

When Jolena answered the door, she was a surprise— much smaller than Lydia had pictured her, eyes the color of the Atlantic, hair as shimmery as fresh snow.

"Yes?"

"Jolena Criggin?"

"Yes."

Lydia pushed back her hair with her sunglasses. "Hello, I'm Lydia. Lydia Porter?"

"Yes?"

"You wrote me a letter?"

"Oh." It took a moment for the woman to remember.

"Oh, yes. *You're* Lydia Porter. I . . . oh, yes. I *did* send you a letter."

Even as Lydia's hope plunged, something else took its place, a thought that ran unbidden through her mind.

Beloved.

As gentle as a nudge.

Beloved, I picked out the color of your eyes, the color of your hair. I sing over you with shouts of joy.

"About the envelope? With one of my old high school tests in it?"

Jolena Criggin narrowed her eyes. "Oh heavens, something Clive left behind."

Lydia felt about fifteen years old. "Yes."

"I have to say, I expected to hear from you via regular mail, Miss Porter. I didn't expect you to arrive at my door."

They were still standing there, and the woman still hadn't invited her in. Well, that was okay. She could say what she had come to say, and leave. "There may be several things about me that you didn't expect."

"I halfway expected not to hear a word from you. It's just a test, after all. Something left over that year from his files."

233

"I'm a high school counselor now," she said. "My time in school made me want to help other kids. Do you know how it is with teenagers"—she didn't know whether to call her *Miss* or *Mrs.*—"Mrs. . . . I-I mean, *Miss* Criggin? Things that seem unimportant to adults can seem disastrous to adolescents."

"Of course they can. Let me get you that envelope. Here. Make yourself comfortable. I'll need to find it." She gestured and held the door.

"Thank you."

The woman disappeared into the back room.

This is the thing, isn't it, God? The reason You let me fall in love with Charlie, the reason everything's in such a mess in Shadrach.

I am still paying for this.

"Here you are." The manila envelope smelled dusty and old. The brad had aged to a rusty green. "There isn't any note in there, Miss Porter. Just that test."

"Thank you."

Lydia sat down and unfastened the brad, half expecting it to break off where she bent it. She turned the envelope up and slid out the pages.

A three-page essay about the motivation of Grendel and Hrothgar in *Beowulf,* written in script that had seemed more than grownup at the time. Each letter of her cursive had been neat and round, with tiny balloon circles dotting each *i.* Beneath her name at the upper left corner of the page and the date, which students had always been required to fill in, he had scribbled a large B+ with his red felt-tip pen.

Lydia held the test to the light. Even the staple had gone rusty. Then, as if she never wanted to touch these pages again, she shoved them back inside. She laid the envelope across her lap and smacked it with two palms. "Thank you."

"It's *Mrs.* Criggin," the woman said. "I remarried almost a dozen years ago."

Their eyes met and held.

When Lydia didn't speak, Mrs. Criggin filled in the silence. "Well, *I* never could figure out what it was for."

I can't do this, God. I absolutely can't—

Oh, Father. Help me. If I walk away from this I'll never have another chance.

She swallowed. Hard. "I think I know," Lydia said, her voice barely audible.

"You do?"

Lydia nodded.

Jolena Criggin waited.

Something whispered in Lydia's heart. *Say it, beloved. Let her see that your hurt is decades deep.*

And the guilt she carried forced its way out.

"I think h-he wanted you and me to meet each other. Because he wanted you to know that everything was my fault."

Silvery eyebrows narrowed. Gentle hands moved, unclasped and then clasped again. "*Your* fault?"

235

Lydia nodded. "About the d-divorce."

"What divorce?"

"Y-yours."

She rocked back. "Mine? Me and Mr. Buckholtz?"

Lydia bit her lower lip and nodded again. Then, "Yes."

The little lady named Jolena Criggin had an odd expression on her face. For a moment, she studied the smooth wooden strips, the pegs, on the floor. When she lifted her face again, Lydia expected to see anger. But instead she saw only regret in the woman's eyes, and a gentle glow.

"What did he say to you, child? I think you should tell me." And in that moment, it might as well have been a decade and a half ago for both of them.

"I-I can't."

"I think you can," Mrs. Criggin said softly. "In fact, I think you're here because you *want* to tell me."

"I'm so sorry," Lydia said instead, and knew she wasn't going to make it.

But her voice stayed calm. She decided to take the envelope and go. She decided this entire day had been for naught. Until something deep inside of her started to rattle loose, to cave in, and the first thing that erupted was tears.

"I'm *so* sorry," she said again. "I am *so sorry.*" And each time she repeated that, her lips went a little thicker. She gave Mrs. Criggin one sane, measured look, said very succinctly, "I'm going to lose it." She pulled her sunglasses down over her eyes even though she was indoors.

And for the first time since Charlie Stains had asked her to marry him, Lydia Porter had a really good cry.

She had no idea exactly when the white linen hanky with the satin-stitch border appeared in her hand. She had no idea how long she sobbed before she could get her mouth around words again. Lydia dabbed her eyes over and over again with the hanky. She swabbed her nose. And finally, finally, the story flowed as fast as her tears.

"I asked him how I did on *this* test." Here she bounced it once on her knee, that very test. "And he said he would tell me if I came to his room after school. And when I did, he was cleaning off the blackboards and I said I would help with the blackboards if he would tell me about my test and he said about my test, it 'depended' and I asked 'Depended on what?' and he said '*This* . . .'"

"Child."

". . . and h-he ran the eraser down my face and shirt. It wasn't the little kind but the big long rubber kind that the janitors use. And he grabbed me and he kept laughing. I thought I'd better laugh, too, like there wasn't anything more fun in the entire world. And he said 'Now there's more chalk on you than on the board' and he rubbed me against him and all I could think of was how much chalk he had on his *nose* . . ."

The handkerchief had been replaced with a box of tissue. "Go on."

"H-he said I made a C but that he thought he was in love with me and if I would come after school like this I would get a better grade on this test and he would get a divorce from you and . . . and . . ."

". . . and you never told anybody about this," Jolena finished the sentence for her.

The Kleenex had diminished to shreds. "I-I was so *ashamed*."

This small, elderly woman, whom Lydia had been direly afraid of not ten minutes before, hugged her the way her mother had never done. Jolena Criggin surrounded her with everything, arms and shoulders and bosom. How wonderful she smelled. Like fresh soap and hydrangeas. How pillow-soft she felt, and how strong. As this woman held her, surrounded her, for the first time Lydia realized that she was surrounded by God's love.

Jolena Criggin rocked Lydia the way Lydia had needed to be rocked when she was sixteen years old, when Lydia herself had thought she was too grown up for such a thing. Lydia hung on to that rocking hug for a long time.

Finally, she said into that soft and wonderful place, "I kept *praying*. And *praying*. And I never went in there again after school. I sat in the back row of class and I always had one of my friends with me. I hid in my room at home and read my Bible and I asked him, 'Father, keep that from happening.' They'd told me that God could do anything when I went to church. I kept thinking, 'How could God let something like this happen because of me?' And so I prayed, 'Don't ever let Mr. Buckholtz get a divorce because of *me*.'"

"And then," Jolena said, "we divorced."

Lydia nodded inside her grasp. "I heard teachers talking in the hall. That's how I found out that he *did.*"

She felt the woman's two small hands, one covering each ear, push her away. Lydia looked up; they met each other eye to eye.

"You have to understand something about Clive, Lydia. Do you think what he said to you was an appropriate thing for him to say? Do you think what he did to you was an appropriate thing to do?"

Shelby's words. Her own words. Intermingled between the past and the present.

I must have wanted it or I would have stopped it somehow. I'm the one to blame.

Each time she had counseled Shelby, she had lifted someone else. Each time she had renounced Shelby's condemning heart, she had allowed the same guilt to sink deeper roots into her own.

He had told her he'd fallen in love with her. Her. And they had to keep it a secret and she had to come to his room and she kept thinking that wasn't the way love was supposed to be.

"I wanted my heart to be pure, and it couldn't be," Lydia told her.

"I want you to know something." With each word she said, Mrs. Criggin jostled Lydia's shoulders with her earnestness. "It wasn't your fault. That was fifteen years ago. It wasn't anything you did."

"I *know* that," Lydia said. "I know that with my words, but not with my heart."

239

"And as far as our divorce was concerned, Lydia. There were other things going on in our lives."

"Mrs. Criggin," she whispered again. "I'm just so sorry."

"For you, child, I want you to live absolved instead of living guilty. We had other things going on or he never would have said the things he said to you in the first place. You weren't the only one that it happened to, you know. In a case like this, there are always others."

In cases like this, there are always others.

There are always others.

That thought took hold of Lydia and burned her like a flame.

Because, if things were really the way they seemed to be in Shadrach, then where were the others?

"I *prayed* so hard." Her voice a wisp, nothing more, talking about the past fifteen years, talking about the past week.

"Well," the woman said. "In your entire praying, dear girl, did you ever stop to think that there might come a moment like this? A moment when a truth breaks through?"

"I don't know."

"Because that's where true healing comes from. I know a heavenly Father who delights in the truth. It is so much more powerful than Him just making something go away."

CHAPTER TWENTY-ONE

In Lydia's old room in the house at Lichen Bridge, Shelby sprawled on the bed while Lydia leafed through the pages of her father's most recent *Reader's Digest*. "I love these stories in here," Lydia said. "'Drama in Real Life.' They are always so unbelievable."

"Next time we stop by 7–11," Shelby said, "I need to get some Blistex or something. My lips are so chapped that they're starting to peel."

"We'll get you some." Lydia turned another page. "If you're desperate enough, there's some in my suitcase. Right there in the zipper compartment to the left of my toothpaste."

"Oh, thanks. I'll put it back."

"You're welcome," Lydia said, focused on the story she was reading about a man who had a heart attack in midflight and his eight-year-old son who had to land the plane.

She heard the sound of the Samsonite opening, the zipper, the hollow tumble of items being pushed around. "It's there," she called out after a minute. "I promise. Keep looking."

Lydia flipped the next page and read more about the desperate landing, the dialogue of the air-traffic controllers to the little boy. She'd almost finished the story before she paused and hollered into the air, "Did you find it?"

No answer from Shelby.

"Shelb?"

And what she saw when she glanced up made her heart freeze.

Shelby stood over her suitcase with a bewildered expression on her face. In her palm rested not only the lip balm she'd been searching for, but a small velvet box from Hocklander's Jewelers as well.

The box stood open. Shelby was staring at the ring displayed inside.

"This is so pretty!"

Their eyes met. Lydia felt her cheeks start burning. What to say to this? Trying her best to sound nonchalant, as if what was inside that box didn't matter, "Yes, it is, isn't it?"

"Miss P?"

"Yeah?"

"What *is* this?"

Words wouldn't come. Lydia laid the *Reader's Digest* upside down on the bedside table.

"Is this what I think it is, Miss P?"

"No. It isn't. Not really."

"Yes, it is something!" And with every word Shelby said, she gestured with the glimmering diamond, the polished gold. "This is an *engagement* ring."

Lydia chose her words carefully, as if she were picking her way down a steep hill, thrashing her way through a tangle of deadfall and underbrush along Viney Creek. "I would like you to put that back where you found it, Shelby. We won't discuss this anymore."

The box clicked shut. *Snap.* Shelby stood over the Samsonite, staring down at it, as if she was buying herself time to think.

"Miss P? Why did you lie to your mom and dad? If you had this, why did you tell them you didn't have anybody in your life?"

"I didn't lie, Shelby. What I said to my parents was completely true."

"But that ring is the most beautiful engagement ring I've ever seen. It's a thousand times bigger than my promise ring. You told them yourself that you weren't dating anybody but you've got this ring. You are."

When you watch a teenager think, it can be a frightening thing, seeing all those cogs turning. Lydia was suddenly terrified by the light flooding Shelby's eyes.

Shelby took a step closer, fear glimmering in her expression. "Miss P." she said very quietly. "I know who it is."

"Oh no, you don't."

"Yes," she said. "I do."

"Shelby, that's okay. I don't want you to—"

"Even if there had been somebody in your life but it hadn't worked, you would have told your mom and dad about it right then. Even if there had been somebody coming for Christmas but now there *wasn't*, you would have said."

"Shelby, it's okay. Please."

"There's only one reason you would have said there wasn't anybody, Miss P, and that is because of me."

"Don't—"

"And that's because there's only one person it could be—"

"You don't know what you're talking about. Shelby, please."

"—and the only person it could be is *him*."

They stared at each other. When she said the word *him* they both knew who she meant.

"You're in love with Mr. Stains, aren't you?"

Jolena Criggin's voice, gently saying this: The moment when truth breaks free.

The next events happened in such a jumble that, later, neither of them would remember in which order they came.

Lydia reaching for Shelby to give her that same sort of hug she'd needed from Mrs. Criggin. Her nodding *yes* against the girl's hair. And admitting the truth, "Yes, Shelby. That's who it is."

Only this one thing. They would only remember this

one thing. And they would each remember it forever: Shelby taking Lydia's hand and saying, "I'm so sorry. I'm so sorry, Miss P." And Lydia reassuring her, "No, Shelby. There isn't anything for you to feel sorry for." But Shelby kept saying it as she began to weep, "Yes, there *is*. *Yes, there is*," her voice awash with anguish. Then, that same desperate, broken expression that had set everything in motion. "I have to tell you the truth, too."

She covered her face with her hands. Then, when Shelby lifted her gaze to Lydia, her face was almost pitifully frightened. "It wasn't him," she said, as tears welled in her eyes.

CHAPTER TWENTY-TWO

*handwritten sign taped to the outside of the office door announced "Miss Porter is out of her office for several days. Anyone needing SAT and ACT study booklets can pick them up from Carol Haucklin, Rm. 103."

Two stacks of pamphlets, still bound in printers' twine, one titled PATHWAYS TO THE FUTURE and another titled BRIDGING THE GAP BETWEEN EDUCATION AND EMPLOYMENT had been tossed on the floor in front of the door.

Friday morning, Mo Eden was preparing for the time when she stepped into health class and taught students how different injuries are caused. Today in her box she carried a dozen local Missouri apples, which she'd bought at a roadside stand, and four hammers, which she'd borrowed from the woodworking room. Today the injury she would teach, using the apples to demonstrate, would be *bruise*.

In that very same woodworking room, the substitute

teacher struggled to help students stay on schedule with their projects. This week the project was constructing a lodgepole pine chair. When the sub had difficulty figuring out how to start the router, Mr. Nibarger had to go in and help.

Sunday morning they would go off Daylight Savings Time. Winter kept moving stealthily closer. The colors seeped earlier from the sky, the jack-oak trees, the old road, and the shadows. And for days the Shadrach students had been passing notes and exchanging clandestine information by their lockers or in the halls, planning their one last bon-fire and party beside the Brownbranch before the weather turned too cold.

Late that afternoon, as darkness moved in soft waves over the knobs and hollows, a group of boys scouted Humbert's Finger, gathering driftwood from where it had floated in on the shore.

And, as often happens when high school seniors get to-gether, plans for pranks began.

"It isn't going to matter," Tommy Ballard said. "Come on. Nothing's going to happen. It'll just be a lot of fun."

"Fun is right. Fun in *jail*."

"You're going to end up in jail just like Stains."

"Nobody's going to get mad at us. Not after what *he's* done. You go after a guy like that, nobody's going to care."

"Could egg the house or something. That would be easy."

Adam Buttars lugged a huge tangle of cedar up and pitched it onto the pile. "Might want to leave it alone. There's been a lot going on around this town."

"Chick*en*."

"The guy deserves it. Come on."

"Sam, of all people, you ought to come with us," Tommy said, his voice quiet but his words boring in. "She's your girlfriend."

"*Was* my girlfriend, until all this."

"See, well, that's what I'm trying to say."

"Okay," Sam said. "I'm in."

౾

EVERY YEAR, each graduating class at Shadrach High School bragged about being the one to invent the gathering. What they didn't know was that these lakeside parties had been going on for over fifty years. Boys and girls both, fresh faced in the waning light, popping dry twigs in half, watching while the wood fibers furled with flame.

This year, a little before dusk on Saturday, kids began to gather on the gravel wash beside the Brownbranch.

Away from the flames, at the edge of darkness, the boys held a meeting.

"You owe me a big one, Ballard."

"What's that?"

"Dad didn't want to let me borrow the truck."

They glanced over their shoulders to see if anybody had heard them. No, didn't seem like it. Everyone else was watching the fire, already talking about marshmallows on sticks.

"You ready?"

"How many trucks we taking?"

"Three."

"Who's driving? You? Devine?"

"You're not taking yours, Buttars. Not unless you got a muffler."

They made each other promise not to use flashlights. They made plans to park two trucks around the corner, get every-body to Stains's house riding in the bed of the third truck.

"You're the one hitching up, Buttars?"

"Yeah."

"We're ready as we'll ever be."

Drivers brandished keys. The others climbed in wher-ever there was room. They headed up the washboards at a good clip, throwing dust, before anyone had a chance to ask them where they were going.

∽

CHARLIE TURNED THE GMC into his driveway after a late meeting with Tuck Herrington. He'd had his share of emo-tions these past few days, but nothing had come close to matching this one. Anger, picking apart his insides like a buzzard.

"Look, Tuck," he'd said. "I will not do this. I'm sorry. I can't."

"It's late, Charlie. I know that. Think about it overnight.

I can still set something up in the morning. It's the weekend, but I can get Judge Foster over the phone tomorrow."

"I'm not going to change my mind tonight. I'm not going to change it in a hundred years." He and Tuck had been children together—Webelos, Mrs. Hammond's third-grade class, the American Legion baseball team—in what seemed like a different lifetime. "I thought you believed in me."

"This has nothing to do with what I believe, Charlie," his friend said. "It has to do with what is legally smart. And *this* is legally smart."

"For you, maybe. Not for me."

"I could get the felony charges dropped. But you've got to agree to this prefiling agreement. You won't have to testify. Neither will she. It will be a lot less messy."

"You don't want me to fight this."

"You plead no contest to two misdemeanor counts of criminal sexual conduct. The charges aren't denied but they're not accepted, either. You get sentenced to a little community service. That's it. It's over. Save your reputation."

"Guess I don't see how telling a judge I don't deny this is going to save my reputation."

"Look, it won't get you your job back. But, at this point, there isn't anything that's going to do that. This will make it end sooner. You can go somewhere else, get a different job. Start your life over. Make people stop talking. And we all know that's the real enemy we're fighting against. People talking."

Charlie had turned around and said it right before he shut the door in Tuck's face: "I am an innocent man, Tuck. Just chalk me up as one of those crazy people who think the truth is more important than what other people say."

Now, turning into his driveway, Charlie had another unpleasant surprise.

Tires had gouged out huge trenches in the front yard. Deep, fat treads had slashed the grass clear past the roots, leaving red soil exposed like a bare wound.

His headlights arced past the blank spot beside the garage.

The kids must be partying at the lake tonight. He knew it for sure because he'd seen the bonfire reflecting on the water.

And someone had stolen his boat.

∽

ONCE THE GANG of boys got back to the bonfire with Mr. Stains's boat, it took them at least five tries to get the trailer backed up to the water. They dented one fender of the trailer on a tree. They bottomed out the axle on a rock in the middle of the two muddy ruts someone had the nerve to call a road. Somewhere along the way they lost the license plate.

They backed one way and the boat went another. They backed the other way, and the boat went straight. Then, like a miracle, as everybody cheered, the boat was unfastened from the trailer and slid smoothly into the lake.

For an hour or so, the students took turns piling people into *Charlie's Pride*. They shoved each other out. They jeered at the ones who swam by firelight toward the shore.

Tommy Ballard was first to discover the cool thing about the light and the fish. He played his flashlight, drawing designs out over the water. The brim beneath the boat followed the beam wherever it pooled.

"Look at these things," he bellowed as he jabbed Adam Buttars in the ribs with his elbow. When he stuck his arm in, he could feel the brim glancing past his skin, flickering away. "They're almost tame. I could catch these with my hands."

"Yeah right, Ballard. Just try."

So he did. He held the flashlight in his teeth and reached in. He caught one.

And then he caught another.

The fish was writhing between his palms when someone shouted, "Hey, there's some man standing over there on the shore. He's shining a light on us. He's gonna see the boat."

Several of the kids on shore began to run. "Get rid of the fish and turn the flashlight off, you doof. Come on, Ballard. Let's get out of here."

"Here, little fishy," Tommy sang out. "Little fishy going to *fly*."

One of the girls screamed, "Don't hurt it," just as Ballard threw it with the same exactness and strength as he would have thrown the last-inning fastball, the last out, to send the Shadrach Legion team into the District playoffs.

The fish hit the man square on the left leg and then foundered its way back into the water. From the distance, a dozen teenagers heard the clatter as the man dropped his fishing pole against the rocks. "No-good *kids*," he bellowed. "Got no business having a party out here."

"Hey, grandpa," Tommy yelled. "Chill. It was just a *fish*."

Sam grabbed Tommy's shoulder. "Hey, take it easy, okay?"

"We got as much business out here as you do," Tommy hollered.

"You got business with that stolen boat?"

"This isn't a stolen boat."

"Ballard, *stop*."

"Funny. It looks just like the one my friend Bartlett donated last month so the church could auction it away. Don't reckon you're the one who bid on it in the auction, are you?"

"Whatever. This boat's *mine*."

The old man started wading out toward them, his lantern high overhead. "You bring in that boat."

Sam tried to stop them both. "Hey, wait. Don't come out here. We'll bring the boat in."

But it was too late. In anger, the man stepped off the shore and surged toward them, sloshing through deeper and deeper water.

"Hey, grandpa. Go back," Tommy yelled. "We'll give back the boat. I was just messing with you."

The boat emptied fast. Everybody bailed out and started swimming, wading, running for shore. The kids scrambled and hid, trying to get away.

Sam was the only one who noticed when the man stumbled and went down.

"Ballard!" Sam shouted from where he was thrashing toward shore. "That old guy's gone under. He fell down or something."

"Did not. He's hiding. Trying to freak us out."

For one night, Sam was finished listening to his friend. "That's where all those old roots are."

Will shouted, "He's got his leg tangled."

"Come on!"

It took precious, long seconds for the boys to find the old man's head and lift it above water.

∞

LYDIA HAD DONE plenty of thinking while she and Shelby had driven home from Lichen Bridge. Thinking how trusting God was the same sort of trust you had to follow when you came down a flight of stairs. Thinking how you put one foot down, knowing the next step was going to be there.

Of course, the return drive had been bittersweet. Lydia was so happy that Charlie wasn't to blame, she could almost forgive Shelby her terrible lie. But to love this girl as much as Lydia had begun to love her also meant to hold her accountable.

"You have to understand what you've done, Shelb," Lydia had said to her. "You've accused an innocent man."

"You wanted me to tell you who it was that day. You kept asking me and asking me," Shelby told her. "I wanted to tell you. But my mother said I could never talk about it to anyone."

"Dearest girl . . ."

"You *believed* me, Miss P. You were the first person who would ever really *listen*."

And Lydia found herself afraid to speak, afraid of what she might say.

"I saw Mr. Stains walking by the window right then outside and suddenly I got *desperate*. His name was the first one I could think of. I knew he would never . . . he would never . . . he's been so nice to me, Miss P; he's the one out of everybody that I could trust."

"Shelby."

"I knew he wouldn't e-ever hurt me."

Regret, as powerful and numbing as anything Lydia had ever known, overcame her.

But why didn't I know that?

Why didn't I think that, out of everybody, Charlie was the one I could trust?

Now, it's too late. I'll always be the one who didn't stand beside him when he needed me the most.

"Every time I told my mother about it, she said she didn't

believe me, that I mustn't talk like that. She wouldn't listen, Miss P. So I was glad when I said it was Mr. Stains, because then she had to hear."

"Shelb, what are you telling me?"

"Kids know how to tell people when it's a teacher or somebody like that. But when it's somebody in your own family, that everybody protects, there isn't anything you know how to say."

Lydia bit her bottom lip and tasted blood. She would wait until the girl was willing to offer more information. She didn't want to make the same mistake twice, trying to push for a name. Lydia gripped the wheel, and wondered if the abuser could be Shelby's uncle, or her real dad, or Tom.

As they made the last turn toward Shadrach and began to round the Brownbranch toward Viney Creek, they passed a car pulled off to the shoulder of the road.

A gleaming white 1976 Pontiac Catalina.

Lydia applied her brakes. There couldn't be another one like that anywhere in St. Clair County.

"Shelb, I think that's your grandfather's car. We ought to stop and make sure nothing's wrong."

"It's okay. We don't have to stop." The girl said it without ever moving her face. She sank down in the seat and stared straight ahead.

"You don't want to?"

"No."

"But, I think we should." Lydia signaled, checked her

rearview mirrors and hung a U. She turned the wheel hand over hand, stunned by Shelby's reaction. "You can wait in the car if you'd like."

"No. Please, Miss P. Would you just *drive?*" Her voice went even more shrill as the car slowed on the gravel. "Please, let's just go."

"Why don't you want to go check on him, Shelby?"

"I just don't."

Lydia braked completely, turned toward her. "You're afraid."

Shelby looked straight ahead. She wasn't panicked, but she wasn't exactly serene either.

"Shelb?"

Shelby crossed her arms and began rubbing the points of her elbows."He . . ." The words came out in a dusty croak. She licked her lips and tried again. "He took all my stuff out of my locker. He came in there to make sure there wasn't anything in there that would make him look bad."

A chill rushed the length of Lydia's spine. Something unimaginable began to form in her head. *Shelby didn't want to go anywhere close to her grandfather.*

When they parked this close to the edge, they could see emergency lights down below. "There is something going on down there, Shelby, but we aren't going to get out of the car, okay?"

"Okay."

"There are people down there taking care of things. We're just going to talk."

"Okay."

Oh, Father, I need Your words. I need Your gentle understanding. If this is what I think it is . . .

And Lydia touched, barely touched, the thing she'd begun to suspect. "So it's your grandfather who's been doing this to you, isn't it?"

Silence.

"You told your mother about your grandfather a long time ago, didn't you? And she said you mustn't talk about it. She said she didn't believe you."

No words came from that side of the seat. Shelby was biting her lip. On her cheeks, the bright flush of shame.

"Is that what happened to you? Is your grandfather sexually abusing you and your mother won't let you tell anyone?"

Shelby, nodding her head. And Lydia, finally knowing.

Because a mother who has to admit that her father had done this to her daughter has to admit that the same person has abused her, too.

CHAPTER TWENTY-THREE

The whole time during Shelby's grandfather's funeral, Sam could not take his eyes off the back of her head. She sat in front of him in the designated family pew of Big Tree Baptist with her hair pulled back in a navy ribbon.

He had caught glimpses of her when she'd first walked into the sanctuary. With her hair like that, wearing that dark navy skirt and standing beside her mother, she looked like she was about eleven years old.

By now, of course, everybody in Shadrach knew what Shelby's grandfather had done. It was lucky that he and Tommy and Will and Adam B. hadn't known about that the night the old man got tangled up in tree roots on the bottom of the Brownbranch. Maybe they wouldn't have tried so hard to save him, to breathe air into his lungs, if they had known.

But, then again, they probably would have tried just as

259

hard. Pastor Joe Douglas was standing beside a closed casket right now talking about forgiveness. He was talking about God, how everybody falls short and that there's nothing anybody can do to make themselves good enough. He was talking about God being a righteous judge who demands the death penalty. He was talking about God being a loving Father who, on the other hand, paid the death penalty for everyone, Himself.

If a person would just be willing to accept that God had given His own son that way. That—because a man named Jesus died—everyone got the chance to ask God questions and to grow close to Him and to feel Him loving them when bad things happened, and when good things happened, too.

That's all you had to do, if you wanted it, was ask.

Sam wondered if Shelby's grandfather had ever thought about that.

At the end of the service, when he brushed past her during the potluck supper, Sam hung back, hoping she would grab his arm.

She did.

"I'm glad you're here," she told him. "It means a lot to me."

"Well," he said, shrugging. "Everybody's here."

He was right. At least thirty Shadrach High School students had come to pay their respects and to show Shelby that they were trying to understand. Even though people were subdued, they still gathered in groups around the room and talked about Lydia Porter and how she'd found a lost baby in the woods.

"I'm sorry about how I acted after the dance," Shelby told Sam. "I shouldn't have run away from you."

"It's okay."

"It was really hard."

"Yeah, I think it would be, too."

"There's some of my friends that are still mad at me, aren't there? For accusing their favorite teacher?"

He nodded. "I guess so. But there are a lot of people who are looking at your side, too, Shelb. They get it. I've heard them talking. It must have been horrible, having somebody in your family do something like that. I've heard people talking in the halls. They said, if it was them, they would have tried to be free of it any way they could. Just the way you did."

They stood there for a minute, looking at each other.

"I've got to do community service for stealing Mr. Stains's boat. We all do."

"What kind of community service?"

"We have to paint all the wooden campground signs down by the lake."

"That doesn't sound like much fun."

"It won't be."

Their eyes met again.

"Tom and Mom say I don't have to go back to school yet, if I don't want to. Since I've already told the truth to Mr. Nibarger and the police."

"Do you want to come back?"

"I don't know."

"What are you going to do?"

"I'm still thinking about that, I guess."

He picked up a napkin from one of the tables and set it back down again. "I don't think you need to stay away too long."

"Why?"

"They're going to forgive you, you know. Since they're so happy that Mr. Stains is coming back."

"But there's just so much—" She stopped again.

"Just so much *what?*"

"You know."

"What?"

She whispered, stepped back, waited. "About me."

For a moment, all that she meant hung in the air between them. "You mean, about what happened to you?"

"Yeah."

He thought about it. "You are who you are, Shelb. That other stuff doesn't make any difference."

"It doesn't make any difference to you, maybe. But it does make a difference to me."

"I guess it would."

"Yeah. And to talk about it, to admit it happened and call it by name. That helps a little bit. I've still got some things to work through."

"I'll miss you until you're there again."

She smiled at him, touched his arm. "It won't be too

long," she said. "Because if you feel that way about it, Sam, then maybe everything's going to be okay."

∽

LYDIA EYED THE IDLING MOTOR on *Charlie's Pride* with no small amount of skepticism. "I'm afraid you'll get me in the middle of the Brownbranch and throw me overboard," she said. "I don't know if I want to go."

Charlie kept his hand on the throttle, ready to power it up.

"You can trust me," he said and, right now, that was no small thing to say. *You can trust me.* "The middle of the lake is a good place to talk."

Beside the Coca-Cola cooler at the marina, Charlie could see Cy shading his eyes and watching them. After everything that had happened to his niece, Cy Porter wasn't letting Lydia out of his sight.

Once she had climbed into his boat and had pointedly strapped herself into a life preserver, Charlie directed them away from shore. "Look, Lydia," he said over the throbbing engine, the churning water. "We've fished enough people out of the brink for one week. This isn't anything that you really need to worry about."

"Okay." She focused somewhere past his left knee. "I'll stop."

"You can drive this thing better than I can, anyway."

She didn't argue with that. "I can."

Charlie knew her well enough to know she'd wait until

they got to Humbert's Finger before she asked any more questions. And he was right. That's exactly what she did. She picked words carefully.

"Are you ever going to be able to forgive her?" she asked.

One beat. Two. "I don't condone the lying. But I think she may have taken the only route that was possible for her to take."

Then, after another long, uncomfortable silence, "Are you ever going to be able to forgive me?"

This was the same question he'd been asking himself for days. Now that it was all over, could they go back to the place they had been? He had to wonder.

Once Charlie had driven the boat to a protected place where the Brownbranch rocked them and the birds serenaded them and the breeze danced over their heads, he cut the engine. "I have to be honest, Lyddie. If we had switched places, I don't know what I would have done."

"That's something you never do know," she said, "until it happens."

A mallard flew overhead, whistling with its wings. They both watched it. He said, "You had to believe her. It was your job."

"Don't let me off the hook like that, Charlie. I had to believe her because I had to believe her. *Somebody* needed to."

"I knew there had to be something behind what she'd

said. That's why I wrote her that note that day. I wanted to talk to her."

"And I stopped you from that, too." Lydia shoved her hands inside her pockets.

"Yes. But you *had* to."

"I'm a different person than I was a week ago." Lydia gazed at the sky. "All of us are."

Charlie hazarded a sharp laugh at that. "Glad you counted me in on that." Another duck flew overhead.

"I can't be everything you wanted me to be, Charlie. I failed you everywhere."

"I've thought about things, Lyddie. How we looked at each other once. How we see each other now."

"Which way do we turn, Charlie? I don't know."

"Maybe it's a bigger test of faith to stand by someone when you have doubts."

"And maybe it isn't. I took the human way out."

"You didn't take any outs at all."

She was silent.

"I have to think about that a lot," he said. "I'm trying to see it through your eyes."

"Now that it's over, I'm not sorry. There are things in Shelby's life that have been brought to light. There are things in my own heart that have been healed."

"Will you tell me?"

"Someday. Maybe when it isn't quite so fresh and tender. In spite of her mistakes, Shelby took me down a road I needed to follow."

"It won't be easy." He ate a sunflower seed out of a bag and spit the hull into the water. "But I still care about you, Lyddie."

"You're right." She stared at the water. "It won't be. But maybe in time . . ."

"I'd like the chance to sort through everything that's in my heart. Will you give me that chance?"

"I'm the one, Charlie, who ought to be asking for second chances."

Charlie was looking at her in an odd way. "You may have saved Shelby, because you stuck by her. Do you realize that?"

"I didn't know I deserved to be cared about the way you care about me, do you know that? I didn't know I deserved to be loved the way *He* loves me."

"Well," Charlie said very quietly, finally reaching across the orange block of life jacket and touching her face. "Now, you do."

"Yes." And her eyes met his head on.

∽

RUMORS FLY FAST in Shadrach because it is the way of every small town. Everyone along Main Street today felt the buzz in the air. Of course the news had started at the counseling office at the high school. Spine-tingling, if it was true.

In the windows at the bank, the tellers counted money with a little less *snap* and a little more smile. Patrice Saunders's dog even got two dog bones at the drive-through window instead of one. Cy Porter, who usually wouldn't leave Viney Creek Marina as long as there was a chore to be done, could be seen mid-afternoon just strolling through town with Jane at his side. Mo Eden carried her basket full of bandages across the road for health class and, when the wind came up and took a few, she laughed and strewed a few more.

Charlie Stains was coming back to work at the high school.

At last he would be able to teach his woodworking students how to complete their lodgepole pine chairs. In spite of the gorilla glue, the chairs that they'd started with a substitute had all collapsed inward within three days.

And maybe they would build another dock somewhere, if Mr. Stains could scout out another one that needed fixing.

Rumor had it that, if Mr. Stains built another dock, Miss P might be along to help. Some people, who had been at the services up at Big Tree Baptist last Sunday, said they'd seen her wearing a ring. Some people said she'd even gotten her fingernails done up because she knew everyone would see.

The kids in Shadrach High School didn't know how they'd feel about that yet. They'd already started talking about how hard it was going to be, remembering to call her Mrs. S instead of Miss P. But who could say how difficult it would really be. Because the Lord had a way of working things out in Shadrach.

∽

BRAD GRITTON HAD his entire class of video students on the front lawn when Lydia Porter and Charlie Stains came out together.

"Okay. Okay," Brad said to his students, his voice raised. "Practice a zoom shot here. Nagle, you need to take the lens cap off or you're not going to get anything. Cassie, I don't think you've got your camera turned on."

"What do we zoom in on?" Cassie asked.

"Anything you'd like. That goose flying up there. The flag blowing in the breeze on top of the flagpole. Anything. Just to get the feel of the video equipment."

While his students began to pan the brick façade of the building, Brad stepped toward Lydia and Charlie.

"Hey," he called, somewhat smugly. "I hear there's good news to report about you two these days."

"Do you?" Charlie asked.

"Yes. I do."

But Lydia didn't say a word to him. She just held out the hand with the diamond engagement ring on it, her eyes reflecting the same sparkle of gratitude that he could see in the stone.

"Congratulations," Brad told her with a somber smile.

After one stretch of awkward silence, in which Charlie glared at Gritton as if he wasn't sure whether he liked him being this friendly with his new fiancée, Lydia couldn't help smiling.

"So Brad," she asked. "How are you doing these days?"

"Okay," Brad said. "But, just okay. Taylor's dad came to pick him up yesterday. So the house is a little quiet right now. Takes some getting used to."

"I'm sorry," she said, and she meant it. She wished Brad the best in the world. "I hope that kid comes back to visit again soon."

"He will, if I have anything to do with it."

"Good."

Brad turned to Charlie. "Say, I hear you applied for a grant to fund your English Lit project at Missouri a few years back. You didn't get it, huh?"

Charlie shrugged his shoulders. "No. One of those tough things. I have a tough time wearing a tie and sitting still in a meeting. I don't play coat-and-tie politics well. Never have. Never will, I guess."

Brad turned back to Lydia. "So now you know. It really was college politics that made Charlie quit university life. It really was college politics that made him come home."

She couldn't resist grinning. They all laughed. "And I am so glad that he did."

As Charlie and Lydia's eyes locked, they forgot all about Brad Gritton standing there or the video class that was in session or the past that they had all struggled through.

The future held a lot of promise.

Charlie bent low and drew Lydia tightly against him. He lowered his lips to hers, claimed her with his kiss.

When he did, at least a dozen video cameras zoomed in.

And, all around the schoolyard, the trees seemed to sing.

AUTHOR'S NOTE

Many times while I was writing *When You Believe*, I questioned God's will. *Maybe nobody's going to want to read about this, Lord,* I said. *Maybe mentioning the topic of sexual abuse is going to offend people.*

But every time I questioned the Father's will for this, He would answer by bringing yet another broken, beautiful, loving, hurt young woman into my life, yet another person who had lived this story.

So many parts of *When You Believe* are true. The story about churchgoers separating into sides at the Sunday service. The story about the woman who said, "Kids know how to tell when it's a teacher or somebody like that. But when it's somebody in your own family, there isn't anything you know how to say." The story of a mother never believing a daughter because, if she admitted the truth, then she would have to admit that abuse had happened to her, too.

Finding God in all of this was a struggle. Often, as I wrote, I felt like the Father was holding me back when I wanted to write something about Him. I did a first rewrite, and a second, without knowing exactly where Lydia's heart was going. Without knowing where *my* heart was going. But then, as I began to discover where my own life ran in the same direction as Lydia's, the pieces began to fit together.

I began to see my own disbelief. Not my disbelief in Him, necessarily, but my disbelief in how God sees me.

For a long time in my life, I wrote Harlequin romance novels. One of my favorite things to do now is explain the course of my career as I moved from writing secular mass-market paperbacks to writing books for the Lord. When I was a teenager, ready to find my own Prince Charming around every corner, my parents teased me about being "in love with love." And it's true. Even now, as I look back at my life, the times when I knew someone was standing beside me, *believing* me, loving me more than I thought I deserved to be loved, those were the times when I felt like my life was soaring with purpose.

How can I give you up, Ephraim? God cries to us. *It was I who taught you to walk, taking you by the arms; but you did not realize it was I who healed you. I led you with cords of human kindness, with ties of love; I lifted the yoke from your neck and bent down to feed you.*

And so, on this last page, I write tonight with much joy. I have discovered, during *When You Believe,* that I am writing books about the greatest romance of all. The Father *created* us to be in love with love. He created in us a need for romance, because that is exactly what He longs to give us. In spite of what our minds tell us to believe, the crusty, hard layers of disbelief have been laying deep and heavy for decades in many of our hearts. We need to let our own unbelief be hammered, chiseled out and assailed by the Word of God. The Father calls us to look not into the mirror of the world, but into the mirror of how He feels about us.

Sometimes knowledge of that love comes in one day. Other times it must be replenished by weeks and months and years of reading and making the Bible your own.

In *When You Believe,* Lydia came to believe a new truth: that she was a one-of-a-kind, irreplaceable, beloved woman to God. That when she sought Him, He shouted over her with joy and sang over her with delight.

The Father wants to be the one you yearn for. He wants to be the one who stands beside you, who gives you confidence, who sets you to soaring with purpose. He *believes* in you. And that ought to change the way you believe in Him. And now that you've read this book, it is my prayer that you, dearest one, will believe in, seek out, and taste His immeasurable, extravagant love for you.

Blessings!

> Deborah Bedford
> P.O. Box 9175
> Jackson Hole WY 83001
> www.deborahbedfordbooks.com

READING GROUP GUIDE

1. When Lydia found out Charlie was accused of abuse, she wondered if she had misunderstood God's will for her life. Why do you think she questioned this? Has there been a time in your life when something you thought God wanted for you didn't turn out the way you expected? Explain.

2. Lydia admitted she didn't think she deserved to be loved the way Charlie loved her. Did Lydia carry guilt and pain from her past that might have made her feel that way? In the end, how was Lydia changed because she questioned Charlie and his love for her?

3. Brad referred to God's love when he said, "But how can something so consistent also be so unpredictable?" (p. 132). What do you think he meant by that question?

4. Lydia prayed, "Oh, Lord. Where are You when You feel

this far away?" (p. 161). Circumstances in our lives can often make us feel like the Father has forgotten us. Has there been a time in your life when you thought this about God? Did you ever come to a place where you understood that He had been closer than you'd thought? Explain.

5. Look up Psalm 1:3. When Lydia saw this Scripture, she finally understood her resentment toward God. What do you think made her see herself in this verse?

6. Cassie Meade showed Lydia a drawing that Charlie judged in an art contest. What was in the drawing? Do you think the author intended this drawing to be symbolic? Where else was this same symbol used in the story?

7. Why do you think the author chose *When You Believe* as the title for the book? What does the title have to do with Lydia and Charlie? What does it have to do with God? With Shelby? With Shelby's family?

8. Why do you think the heavenly Father allowed Lydia to confront the pain from her own high school years?

9. When Lydia heard God's voice, He said, "Use the sledge-hammer of My Word to chisel away your hurt" (p. 223). Find verses in the Bible that you think might have helped Lydia. Start with Hebrews 13:6, Isaiah 41:10, and Jeremiah 31:13. Keep the Scriptures marked so you can use them to pray God's Word over members of your group who need encouragement.

If you liked *When You Believe . . .* be sure to pick up *Remember Me.*

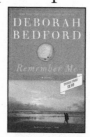

Sam Tibbits loves life—especially life at Piddock Beach, where his family spends its summer vacations. It is here where he first meets Aubrey, a local girl who becomes his childhood confidante . . . and later, his first love. So the year Aubrey's family moves away with no forwarding address, Sam is crushed. He was going to propose.

Aubrey McCart enjoys being with Sam. He accepts her unconditionally like her father never has. But when her father's pride and joy—her brother—is killed in Vietnam, Aubrey is unable to cope. She chooses a path that changes her life forever, leading her away from Sam.

Years later, when Sam and Aubrey find themselves back at Piddock Beach, the two are forced to confront their abandoned friendship and make peace with their lives. But can they do so without following a path that could devastate both of them forever?

Available now wherever books are sold.

Also, be sure to check out
A Rose by the Door!

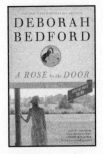

Every summer, visitors come to Bea Bartling's home in Ash Hollow, Nebraska, to see the historic yellow rosebush that served as a famous trail marker for wagons on their way west. And every night Bea prays she will find a special face among those at her door. Then she gets crushing news that the son who ran away years ago has been killed. Overwhelmed by grief—and bitterness as hard as steel—she has no welcome in her heart and no room in her life for the woman and child who soon show up at her door. Yet their arrival changes everything.

Now, as old secrets are revealed, a lonely woman discovers that a prodigal son may still come home if she accepts a precious gift of grace—and if she dares to believe in the miraculous power of love.

Available now wherever books are sold.

And don't miss
A Morning Like This

David and Abby Treasure seem to have everything together: a perfect marriage, a perfect son, and a perfect life.
But one simple phone call turns their world upside down.
Years ago, David had an affair outside of his marriage and,
though he never knew it, the affair produced a daughter.
Now his former lover calls with heartbreaking news: his
daughter is dying of leukemia. Her only hope for survival
is a bone marrow transplant—from David or his son.

Can David and Abby set aside their betrayal and anger to
save a little girl's life? If they can make it through, they may
find that their live for one another and their faith in God
can be redeemed . . . and grow stronger than ever before.

Available now wherever books are sold.

And you'll love the *New York Times* bestselling novel *The Penny*!

Jenny Blake has a theory about life: Big decisions often don't amount to much, but little decisions sometimes transform everything. Her theory proves true in the summer of 1955, when fourteen-year-old Jenny makes the decision to pick up a penny imbedded in asphalt, and consequently ends up stopping a robbery, getting a job, and meeting a friend who changes her life forever.

Jenny and Miss Shaw form a friendship that dares both of them to confront secrets in their pasts—secrets that threaten to destroy them. Jenny helps Miss Shaw open up to the community around her, while Miss Shaw teaches Jenny to meet even life's most painful challenges with confidence and faith. This unexpected relationship transforms both characters in ways neither could have anticipated, and the ripple effect that begins in the summer of the penny goes on to bring new life to the people around them, showing how God works in the smallest details. Even in something as small as a penny.

Available now wherever books are sold.